CREED

KINGS OF CARNAGE

WALL STREET JOURNAL & USAT BESTSELLING AUTHOR

GLENNA MAYNARD

Creed ©2024 Glenna Maynard

Cover Design: CT Cover Creations
ISBN: 9798303407688

CREED

My little hellcat is all grown up.
Creed

As the Road Captain for the Kings of Carnage Motorcycle Club I've earned a reputation as a shameless womanizing force to be reckoned with. When the brat who once made my life hell calls me in utter terror, I know that this will be the ultimate test of my strength and my heart. It's been ten years since I last laid eyes on Lottie. When my gaze lands on a gorgeous raven-haired beauty with a banging body the last thing I expect to see is her baby blues staring back at me. Nor do I anticipate the wild ride that ensues. She's in trouble and I'm the only man who can save her.

Lottie

Someone is stalking me and when they break into my apartment, I know I can't face this on my own. In fear for my life, I make the one call I never thought I'd be forced to place to Creed. My older, hot as hell outlaw stepbrother I've always had a crush on. I'm no longer that spoiled girl he remembers. I've grown up and am ready to lay it all on the line. My life and my heart are in his hands.

Alabama officers: Hilary Storm (Havoc), Sapphire Knight (Tyrant), Glenna Maynard (Creed),Chelsea Camaron (Rogue) may love always find you

CHAPTER ONE

Lottie

THE PAST

"What if we get caught?"

"Isn't that part of the thrill?" Seth grins at me with his panty dropping smile. The one that got me into this position. In his room. In his bed. Doing naughty things that we shouldn't. Since the day we met, all I've wanted is this. His lips on mine.

We're dirty and wrong.

I'm his secret.

He calls me his hellcat.

His heaven and his hell.

Because no one can know about us.

One day, we'll really be together. And everyone will know that I'm his girl.

When his friends are around, he pretends to hate me and messes around with other girls.

When it's only us, he's sweet.

I wish it could always be like this.

The two of us, alone in this room. A space where no one else exists.

Present Day

"Are we still on for tonight?" Tonya smirks deviously at me as she undoes the strings of her apron and tosses it into her locker.

"I don't know." I straighten my ponytail and test my pen on my order pad, wondering if Tonya swapped our pens again when I wasn't paying attention. She's always stealing my good ones.

"What do you mean you don't know? Don't be a sourpuss and wuss out on me. This is the first night I've had a babysitter in months, and I want to go watch hot dudes pummel the shit out of each other." She swaps out her work shoes for flats. Tonya worked the breakfast and lunch rush, and I came in about halfway through her shift to work the split shift.

I'm just happy I'm not stuck on closing, but I still have another three hours.

"Don't tell me you're still pining after that asshole biker." I scrunch my nose.

"No, but if he is there and wants to give me a ride on that purple headed monster then..." she shrugs.

"Never call sex that again. Please and thank you."

"Pfft. Whatever. I'll be expecting you at my place. You can wear something of mine. None of your stuff is slutty enough for where we're going tonight." She flashes me a dazzling smile that is normally reserved for male customers she's hoping to earn a big tip from.

"Yeah. Yeah. I'll be there." Tonya knows how I feel about hanging around bikers.

They remind me of my former stepbrother. When our parents were married, he was always tinkering with his motorcycle or getting into fights. He stayed in trouble. So much so that all our parents did was fight about what to do with him.

He's probably in jail if he's not dead.

I shake off those old memories. The last thing I want to do is reminisce about the past or Seth. He's long gone and has been out of my life for nearly a decade.

"Perfect. Don't be late." Tonya gives me a little wave and exits the back door with her purse slung over her shoulder.

"Order up," Carl shouts from behind the counter, signaling that my break is over.

I arrange steaming hot plates of food on the tray. The scent of burning bacon and freshly brewed coffee permeates the kitchen of Trish's Diner. A busy restaurant that's a second home to me with how much time I spend here.

I glance at myself in the reflection of the glass cooler reserved for the creamer and orange juice. My lipstick is long gone, and my eyeliner could use a touchup.

Ugh. Looking haggard isn't going to earn me any decent tips, and I could use the money. Tonya has mentioned my moving in with her a few times to make life more affordable for the two of us, but I prefer to be on my own.

I nod before balancing the tray above my shoulder with one hand so I can weave my way through the crowded tables without any incidents. The five o'clock early dinner crowd has hit. I'm in for another busy evening of serving country fried steak dinners to flirty truckers and worn-out locals looking for a hot meal and a familiar smile.

"Here you are, folks," I announce, mustering as much fake cheer as possible, placing plates in front of a couple who dine together every evening like clockwork. Janice and Leonard. He's the county attorney, and she's the vice principal at the elementary school. They always order the same thing. "Enjoy your meals."

"Thanks a bushel," Janice replies, her eyes crinkling thoughtfully at the corners as she cuts into her grilled lemon pepper chicken. Her companion grunts in his agreement, already too busy inhaling his burger to bother with making polite conversation.

Watching the two of them, I wonder if I'll ever find my person.

"Can I get a to go box?" someone from table four calls out.

The remainder of my shift continues in much the same way, a blur of orders and conversations dotted by wise-cracks and the occasional spilled drink or dropped food sticking to the bottom of my antislip shoes. Waiting tables isn't exactly glamorous, but it pays my rent and keeps my mind off my recent breakup with Cade.

Which is the only reason I'm going out with Tonya tonight. I need to stop moping around over that asshole.

By the end of my shift, I'm dead on my feet. What I really want is to go straight home, but I'll never hear the end from Tonya if I bail on our plans.

I don't bother changing out of my work clothes. Tonya will just want me to swap my outfit for one of hers when I get to her place. I make the drive to her apartment across town. The opposite of where I live. She lives in an in-come-based unit. Considering her ex-husband never pays for child support, she needs all the help she can get. I know splurging on a sitter is a rare treat for her. It's why I always give her cash for her birthday and Christmas.

The woman has what she calls mom guilt. Meaning, any extra money is almost always reserved for her daughter. I park in the guest spot and walk up the stairs to her apartment. The sound of Elmo screeching from her TV fills the breezeway and I smile.

Tonya's ex-husband might be a piece of crap in the dad department, but he fathered the cutest little girl in the world. When he found out that Kaydence had down syndrome, he claimed she wasn't his. Dude is a real loser. Tonya and Katydid are better off without the asshole in their lives. Luckily, Tonya's mom watches her when she can't afford to send her to daycare. And when I can, I pitch in.

I knock twice, and the sitter comes to the door. "Hey, Lottie. Tonya's in the bathroom doing her hair."

"Thanks, Brenda." She's an older woman who used to work with us at the diner but retired last year. She watches Kaydence when Tonya's mom needs a break or when Tonya doesn't want her mom to know she's going out. Linda has this weird attitude about Tonya getting involved with anyone. She's mostly being cautious about anyone potentially coming into Kaydence's life, but Tonya deserves to be happy.

I greet Kaydence with a smile, and she returns squirming around and dancing to Elmo.

Tonya is in the bathroom spraying enough hairspray over her bottle red hair to choke a horse.

"Good. You're here."

"I promised I would be."

"I laid your clothes on the bed. Did you bring shoes?" She spares me a glance as I wave a hand in front of my face, trying to escape the sticky cloud as she does another round of spritzing her curls.

I dart down the hall before I die from ingesting all those chemicals. She can't be serious. There's a little black dress slung across the foot of her bed. There's not enough material to cover my ass, let alone the rest of my torso.

With a sigh, I move to her closet and start sliding the hangers across the rack, hoping to find something that won't reveal everything the good man upstairs blessed me with.

"Get out of my closet and put on the dress," Tonya snaps at me.

"Oh, is that what you call that scrap of fabric? I thought it was for Kaydence."

"Ha. Ha. It stretches. I'll have you know."

I arch a brow at her. "Uh huh. Sure it does," I tell her, my tone heavy with skepticism like my facial expression isn't giving me away. "Is there enough time for me to hop in the shower and wash the stink of grease off my ass?"

"If you don't wash your hair and you stop arguing about the dress and trust me."

"Fine."

She smiles, satisfied, thrusting the slinky dress into my arms. "Now get to gettin'."

"I'm going. I'm going." I could be rude and take my time long enough to make us late, but I won't do that to Tonya. I rush into the shower and start scrubbing. I know that being on her own gets stressful, and she needs this night out. We both do, really. My mind drifts back to Cade. The prick who ghosted me. One day, he simply stopped calling me. His number was disconnected, not even a full day later. The jerk vanished without a word. The first week I was afraid something terrible had happened to him, but I guess he forgot we were friends on social media, and I could see he was active, mostly late at night. Then I spotted his car around town. He could have broken up with me like a normal person.

I towel off and slip on the dress. Tonya wasn't wrong. The material stretches and sticks to all the right places. I wish Cade could see me in this. I'd tell him to eat his heart out.

I redo my ponytail and freshen up my makeup. If I'm going out, I might as well give my full effort to look damn good.

Who knows what the night will bring?

As soon as I park, unease fills me. There's a sea of motorcycles lined up in front of the entrance of what is normally an abandoned gymnasium that was part of the old high school before they built the new one closer to the freeway. Tonya and her love of men who ride will be the death of me. She grins big, staring at her phone.

"Wait until you see Ghoul's friend."

"Wait what? You didn't mention anything about meeting his friend."

"You can thank me later," she practically squeals. "He's fit as fuck. You'll see."

Reluctantly, I follow Tonya into the fray. She grabs my hand, rushing through the growing crowd. My belly does a dip. Heat flashes up the sides of my neck.

This is what I get for coming to the city with her.

Bikers and violence.

At least they are pretty to look at with their tattooed, slicked up bodies. Weaving our way through the energetic crowd, we end up at a makeshift bar selling overpriced plastic cups of tap beer. "Two please." Tonya hands the man ten bucks.

"None for me," I tell her as she tries thrusting one of the piss hot beers into my hands.

"Come on. One drink won't kill you."

"Maybe not, but I'm driving," I remind her.

"Fair enough. I'll give it to Ghoul. He said he'd be in the back by the locker rooms."

"Great," I mutter to myself. Ghoul isn't one of my favorite people. The dude only uses Tonya as a booty call when he rolls into town every few months. His friend will be sorely disappointed when he realizes I'm not down for a one nighter. I don't care how hot the guy is. The knowledge that he's a buddy of Ghoul's is all the confirmation I need that he probably sucks, too. I'll probably bail the second Tonya links up with the jerk.

I'm not interested in becoming a notch on some stranger's bedpost or inviting him back to my apartment.

CHAPTER TWO

CREED

Feet pounding the pavement, each step echoes in the park's quiet as sweat drips down my back. I've got a job to do. Antarctica by $uicideboy$ blares through the speakers of my earbuds. The weight of my responsibility and my duty to the club, Kings of Carnage, rests on my shoulders. I'm the Road Captain and take my position seriously. My patch is a badge of honor. One I wear with pride and have inked on my back.

My loyalty to the club comes before all else.

An incoming call vibrates from my pocket, but I ignore it. It's not the club and I have to focus. The pay day on this particular job is one I can't afford to pass up. I'm not worried, but that doesn't mean I can afford any distractions. If I'm going to pay off the build on my cabin, I've gotta make this happen.

My cell goes off again, alerting me to a new voice mail. Probably Ember checking up on me. She was probably the last woman I was even close to being serious about until life reminded me we weren't meant to be. I ran away from her like the room was on fire when she told me she was pregnant with Smoke's child. I knew the score between us. She was always going back to him, and I had a life to get back to.

We weren't meant to last.

I filled a role for her, and she gave me something beautiful to cherish when I think about her. With her dark hair, blue eyes, and pouty lips that always felt familiar. It was her eyes that first drew me to her. Those haunting eyes filled with such beauty and sadness, burning with desire. She would never be mine. She had an ache, and I was her temporary remedy.

I did her a favor, and she rewarded me with her vulnerability.

My only regret is the way I dropped her like a bad habit, but things happen the way they are meant to. I had a new job. A new target to take out. Ember couldn't come with me.

As soon as I got shot of her, I was back on the road. I left Anarchy, California, and booked it to a bar in the middle of nowhere called the Velvet Rooster to pick up my intel. Over a year later, I'm still doing the same shit.

Avoiding relationships.

Killing for money.

I'm a killer for hire.

A professional hitman.

Not exactly what I dreamed of when I was a kid, but here I am.

Most people, when you ask them what they are good at, say something like I'm good with a wrench or computers or something. Me? I'm good with my fists. Learned early in life to defend myself from assholes like my old man who liked to get drunk and slap their family around. If you ask my father, his memory differs vastly from mine.

In his eyes I was a troubled little shit with mommy issues.

Maybe I was, but he was still a lousy father. He's always hated me because I have my mother's smile, and she didn't want him. Still can't mention them to each other. Too much bad blood. They divorced when I was five and when she left, she didn't take me with her. Bounced between my grandmother's and different relatives until my father married my stepmother. God rest her soul. She tried to mother me, but I was too old for that shit by the time she entered my life with her brat of a daughter, Charlotte. Aka Lottie. My terror of a stepsister who loved to make my life hell.

She was tempting and gorgeous.

Off limits.

But I couldn't resist the challenge of conquering the forbidden. Sneaking around with her. Stealing kisses. Loving the thrill making her mine gave me. Until my father found out and put me out on my ass. I left Lottie a note asking her to come with me. When she didn't show up at the park, I knew she'd made her choice, and it wasn't me. It was probably for the best, but that shit was my first real heartbreak.

All that stuff feels like it was a lifetime ago. Sharon passed away about ten years ago. Was the last time I spoke to my old man or Lottie. If you could call it speaking.

My actual family never wanted me, so I found my own with the guys I grew up with. We've always had each other's backs. I won't let them down.

Not then.

Not now.

Not ever.

I run another lap around the park, waiting for my target. He has a schedule that he sticks with, like clockwork. Every morning, he jogs around this park. Alone. Unprotected, unsuspecting. A man like him only fears what people would think of him if they knew the truth. He's a functioning alcoholic who loves to take out his frustrations on his wife with his fists.

Reminds me of my own father. A real bastard.

When I crack his skull on the pavement, it will appear like a freak accident and his poor wife will collect the hefty life insurance policy. She's earned it for all the abuse she's endured by his hands. Stupid fuck will never see it coming.

When the police investigate, they'll suspect he tripped on the fallen wet leaves due to the worn tread of his running shoes.

Sometimes it's almost too easy.

Almost.

He rounds the corner of the path, tripping like I knew he would over the wire, unable to stop himself due to his brisk speed. His eyes meet mine on the way down, his lips curving into a shocked expression. A perfect O, ready to scream. I crouch down next to him as his head is about to bounce off the pavement, placing a jagged rock with a sharp edge there to meet him. Like I said, it is almost too easy. An unfortunate accident.

Once he ceases breathing in this world and I'm back at the clubhouse, I check my voicemail after my shower.

"Fuck me, man. Can you send someone to pick me up? Where do you live again?" Ghoul asks some chick and repeats the address to the fucking clubhouse.

Fucking idiot.

I dial him back.

"You've got Ghoul. I'm balls deep in your mom's snatch. Leave a message."

Like I said. Idiot.

In the comfort of my bed, I kick back, and doom scroll social media. Ember posted new pictures of the baby. My heart cracks slightly at the images. If things had been different, they coulda been mine. I want a family someday, just not currently. I heart react to the images and leave her a comment. 'Happy looks good on you, beautiful.'

My comment isn't an empty sentiment. I am happy for her and Smoke. Even if I think he's a prick who doesn't deserve her. I've gotta get past that shit. He won. I should have brought one of the bitches that hang around to my room to blow me. Instead, I'm in my room like some poor sap, feeling sorry that I haven't moved on since my road trip with Ember.

Twilah Jane is always down to fuck even though she likes to play it like she's shy. Bitch is a freak and would smother gravy on my dick and lick it off if I'd let her. Then there's Darlene with her flat ass and Kitty with her pierced cunt. Slim pickings. But that's what you get in a piss poor town with one fucking street.

I think even the prospects have fucked all three of them by now. I like to get off as much as the next man, but I'm tiring of convenient pussy.

I need the thrill of the chase.

Someone who challenges me and won't put up with my bullshit.

A woman who gets under my skin, not makes it crawl because all my friends have already fucked her. My cell lights up with another call. This time its Ember and I send her to voicemail. I know she worries about me, but it's time to cut the cord. She's another man's Ol' Lady. I can't move forward if I'm staying tethered to the past.

Placing my phone on silent, I roll over and try to get some sleep. The last thing I need is to show up at tonight's fight unrested.

I bounce on the balls of my feet, throwing practice jabs in the air.

"Looking good, brother." Ghoul grins, plopping down on one of the benches of the locker room. "Big fucking crowd."

I nod and roll my shoulders, trying to keep myself psyched up. Not that I take much to get going. I just imagine every opponent I face is my fuckface of a father. I'm sure a therapist would have a field day with my trauma and how I choose to deal with it. Fucking and fighting. My two favorite pastimes.

"Got you a real sweet piece lined up for later. Tonya has this friend." Ghoul lets out a whistle. "Smokin' body on this bitch. I'd try to get in there if I wasn't fucking her friend and thought she'd be down."

"One day you're going to poke the wrong bear."

He shrugs. Dumb fuck has no fear. In my experience, there's no one more savage than a scorned woman.

"You haven't met this chick yet. On a scale of one to ten, she's fucking fifteen."

"If Selena Gomez isn't out there, I'm kicking your ass," I joke.

"Trust me." He slicks his shaggy hair back off his neck and into a bun.

"Last time I trusted you, I woke up to my wallet gone and my couch on fire."

"It wasn't that bad. I got your wallet back."

"Yeah, and it was five hundred dollars lighter."

"Want to see her picture?"

"No. I don't need the distraction."

"I can take a hint. I'll see you out there. Give'm hell, man."

I shake my head. Fucking love Ghoul like a brother, but trouble follows that fucker everywhere he goes.

CHAPTER THREE

Lottie

"You down for a three-way?" Ghoul questions and wags his tongue at me like a dog. He's disgusting. Physically, he's not bad looking. He's a little rough around the edges in that bad boy kinda way. Facial hair, longer hair, tattoos. It's when he opens his mouth that he ruins it.

Tonya laughs it off, smacking his chest.

The fights haven't even started yet and I'm ready to ditch this scene. I can't stand this dickhead. Tonya could do so much better. She literally has the worst taste in men.

"So tell me about this friend of yours." I change the subject. I'm already here. I may as well see how this plays out. Who knows? Maybe the guy will at least be hot.

"My man is a beast. He's going to love you. You're just his type."

"And what's that?"

"Dark hair. Blue eyes. Nice rack." Tonya elbows him in the ribs at the last remark.

"What's he do when he's not pummeling the shit out of someone?"

19

"Works on the road a lot."

"Is he like a lineman or something?"

"Yeah. Something like that."

My stomach sinks. I know not all men who work on the road cheat on their significant other, but the percentages aren't favorable. Not that it matters. It isn't like I expect to hit it off with this dude, whoever he is. I've not even laid eyes on him and already I'm imagining all the worst-case scenarios, like we're getting married, and he's determined to break my heart. I'm being ridiculous. I've always been this way. My brain is wired to automatically assume the worst about everyone. If I expect the worst, then I can't be disappointed when people eventually fuck me over. I let my guard down with my ex and I have no plans to get burned again.

"You'll love Creed."

With those words, my heart drops to my feet and splinters wide open as a rush of emotions slams into me. My first kiss. My first everything was all with Seth Creed. Most of all, my greatest heartbreak. "Did you say Creed?"

Music blares from some speakers near the makeshift ring. The crowd erupts in a roar of cheers and expletives. Ghoul ignores my question. It's possible I heard him wrong. He could have said Reed.

Bile churns in the pit of my stomach, threatening to race up my throat. The only Creed I know is Seth Motherfuck-ing Creed. My jerk of a stepbrother. I should say ex-stepbrother since our parents divorced before my mother passed away.

He can't be the only guy in the world people call Creed. Last I knew, he wasn't even living in this state. And yet my heart flutters at the thought of seeing him after all these years. I knew it was wrong to crush on him when I was just a kid. He was older, hot, and dangerous. The bad boy type that you're well aware you can't fix but would give anything for the privilege to simply try.

And God, did I try to save him from himself.

In the end, I failed.

My love wasn't enough.

I wasn't enough.

I followed him and his friends everywhere. Got him in trouble many times because I was jealous of the girls he was fooling around with. I was never the kind of girl he'd ever look at, even if he wasn't older than me. Back then, I was still fat and wore glasses. Then one day he looked at me like he could see past my weight and insecurities.

He looked at me like maybe he loved me. At least that's the lie I fed myself when I'd go into his room and give myself to him in any way he wanted. I craved him until one day he was simply gone. He left without a goodbye, and when I did see him again, he fucked my best friend after my mother's funeral.

It wasn't until months after my mother passed away that I started dropping my weight and caring about styling my hair and wearing makeup.

None of that matters now. It's all in the past.

Seth Creed is the past. And so is Cade.

And yet I can't help but wonder where Seth is. How he turned out. If he found that beautiful life, he was always talking about having one day. What a foolish girl I was to dream that I'd be a part of that life. That when he talked about leaving, I thought he meant with me.

Sucking in a deep breath, I watch as the first contender is announced. Relief and disappointment both flood me at the realization this guy isn't my Creed. I shouldn't want to see him.

But I do.

I want him to see how I've shed my weight and lost my glasses except for when I'm vegging out at home. The rest of the time, I wear contacts. Especially when I'm working.

I want him to see with his own eyes that I've survived life without him.

That I didn't need him.

Even if I wanted him.

The pain thoughts of him brings burns through me like a ring of fire. Threatening to consume me and suck me back under.

They say we only get one great love.

He was supposed to be mine.

Blinking slowly as if coming out of a daze, I return to the now desperate to escape those old wounds that linger in the back of my mind.

"Fighting out of the blue corner, welcome to the arena, Rage."

"Oh no, Tonya," mutters, her face stricken with horror. "I can't be here," she whispers to me as Ghoul chats with some other biker. The name on his cut says Rogue. He catches my eye and grins at me, but I don't think he recognizes me. I'd know that smile anywhere because he was always hanging with Seth.

Which can only mean one thing.

He's here.

I shouldn't be surprised that he still hangs with the same crew or that they belong to a motorcycle club. I shift my attention back to Tonya as she shakes her head back and forth. "What's wrong?"

"My ex. That's what."

"Husband?" My eyes nearly bug out of my head as I look back at the guy they call Rage. I've only ever glimpsed him in old pictures from Tonya's Facebook page. The guy is huge and totally ripped.

"Do you want to leave?"

"Why do you look like someone just kicked your puppy?" Ghoul asks, wrapping an arm around her waist, kissing her neck.

"Fighting out of the red corner. Welcome to the arena, Creed!" The deep voice booms over the microphone.

I gulp and watch my past and present collide. Seth Creed's arms are thicker and more inked than I remember. His murderous expression is focused on the man in the gray shorts who is staring at Ghoul like he wants to pound him into hamburger.

Tonya squeezes my arm, digging her nails into my skin in crescent-shaped grooves.

"What the fuck?" Ghoul mumbles as Rage charges straight for us, yelling, "You whore!"

I yank Tonya out of her ex's path as his fist connects with Ghoul's jaw.

All hell breaks loose. Everyone around us is screaming and throwing punches. I lose hold of Tonya as she lurches herself forward and climbs on Rage's back like a flying monkey of chaos.

"Fuck you, Mateo. Fuck you." She cries and hits him on the back of the head.

Another biker gets hold of Tonya as I'm shoved to the ground in the mayhem.

I'm down on all fours, hoping my ass and breasts aren't hanging out of this teeny dress and that I'm not about to be trampled.

"Are you okay?" A deep voice sends shivers throughout me as I stare up into a pair of green eyes I could never forget.

My words refuse to leave my tongue as we continue to gaze at each other.

Time seems to stop and all the noise and fighting blurs into the background.

I can scarcely breathe as Seth Creed stares at me like he wants to devour me.

My body and my heart remember all too well what that feels like.

His taste. Cinnamon toothpaste and sin. His touch. Rough and greedy.

"Do I know you?" His lips curve into an intrigued smile.

Not this version of me, I want to tell him yet refrain. He doesn't recognize me. My heart cracks in two and I do my best to mask my disappointment.

I don't respond but accept his offered hand. "Thanks," I answer, praying he didn't notice the way my knees wobbled on my way up.

"Name's Creed." He waits a beat for me to reply. "And you are?" he presses.

"Sorry, I've gotta go. Tonya?" I step around him as the crowd further separates me from my friend.

Seth smiles bigger as he blocks my path once more.

"Don't you have a fight to get back to? Faces to punch or something?"

"Nah. That dumbass just forfeited his part of the purse." He licks his bottom lip. "Want to get out of here?"

"Not with you."

He rewards me with a deep belly chuckle that sends me back in time to when our lives were so different, but connected.

"You going to keep pretending?" he states, but the words come out in question.

My pulse thrums against my temples as he continues to stare at me, and I wait for him to work my identity out.

"Maybe I have one of those faces." I make my way to where Tonya is struggling against the arms of a large man as Creed and an even larger guy with just as much ink as him separates Ghoul and Tonya's ex.

"You okay?" I ask, though I already am aware she's anything but fine.

"What gives him the right? Where does he get the fucking audacity?" She shudders and bursts into tears.

"Oh, honey."

The biker holding her back releases her into my hold, and I wrap my arms tight around her. "You want to get out of here?"

Tonya sniffs and wipes her nose with the back of her hand. "Is my makeup ruined?"

I swipe the pads of my thumbs under her eyes, removing her smudged eyeliner. "Good as new."

My bestie squares her shoulders, pushing her chest out. "He doesn't get a say in who I fuck." She marches through the part of the crowd, going toward where Ghoul and her ex-husband are separated. Flipping Kaydence's father off,

Tonya then wraps an arm around Ghoul's neck, pulling him in for the world's most sensual kiss.

Rage or whatever his name is stomps off, shoving people out of his way.

Creed whistles and I give Tonya a wave.

Time for me to go.

"Lottie," my name is called in a growl, and I freeze in place, closing my eyes at the sound of his voice.

He remembers and part of me wishes he wouldn't. His tattooed hand grips my hip and the heat of him washes over me from behind.

"Where do you think you're running off to, hellcat?"

I spin around at his use of the nickname he gave me years ago. "Don't call me that."

"All right then. What should I call you? Liar?"

"What?"

He licks his lips, and my brain instantly wants to know how they'd taste. "Back there. I asked you your name and if we knew each other. Why'd you lie?"

"You had no clue who I was?"

"Bullshit. Like I could ever forget you. Why'd you lie to me?"

My heart stutters in my chest. *Like I could ever forget you.* "Because I wanted to avoid this conversation."

"You mean the one about how you threw yourself at me the last time we saw each other after you were the one who ended things?"

"Can we pretend that never happened?" Tears threaten to fall as my cheeks burn. "I never ended things. You ran away."

"I'm not the only one who disappeared."

"I'm not talking about this."

"That's where you're wrong. What the fuck was up with that?"

"I was drunk and grieving and you were there. I was embarrassed. After."

"Fair enough."

"Are we done here?"

"Not even close."

Chapter Four

CREED

"We're done." Lottie throws me her sass. Used to, her bitchy attitude rubbed me wrong. Tonight though, I'm finding that attitude of hers hella sexy.

"Come back to the clubhouse. Have a drink with me." I thought I'd worked her out of my system years ago but seeing her face to face. Nah. All those old wounds are still fresh.

"That's a terrible idea."

"What else are you going to do?"

"Get a good night's sleep."

"One drink, hellcat."

"I told you to stop calling me that."

"What's the matter? Afraid you might have a good time?"

Her pretty blues roll heavenward. "What's the point? We're not friends. Hell, I'm not sure if you even like me. We're strangers now, you and me."

"Been years, Lottie. I'm sure we've both changed." She's certainly changed physically. Not that she needed to. Even when she had some weight on her, she was just as beautiful. She was my greatest temptation. My heaven and hell. I wanted her but couldn't have her. Not in the way I wanted back then.

She blows out an exasperated laugh. A soft but sweet noise that warms me in places, the honeyed sound shouldn't after all this time has passed. "Fine. One drink."

There's no way she's climbing on the back of my bike with that slip of a dress she's wearing. For one, it wouldn't be safe. Second, I don't want her flashing her ass to everyone.

"Bring your friend. She knows the way."

What the fuck am I doing? Am I really flirting with Charlotte? The girl I've loved to hate.

No one knows her better than I do. I don't care if it's been ten years since we fucked each other over. I had to walk away. I was nineteen, and she was only sixteen at the time. Everything about the two of us was wrong.

But that was then, and this is now.

I watch her as she saunters over to her friend, swaying her hips, having no damn clue how good she looks doing it. I must be losing my goddamned mind. This is a terrible idea. Nothing good will come from this. She's always been off limits and too damn good for me. So why does that make me crave her? Want to consume her. Act out every filthy fantasy playing through my mind each time I stare into her big blue eyes. What I wouldn't give to taste her forbidden lips once more. My blood rises to the surface as she laughs at something Havoc just said to her.

Her gaze meets mine and her cheeks bloom a pale shade of pink.

Lottie is the one who got away. I've told myself it was for the best, but now I'm not so sure.

At the clubhouse, Lottie sits next to me. Eyes downcast, she grips the neck of her beer bottle, doing her best to avoid having any close contact with me. When she looks at me, it's almost as if she's afraid I'm going to disappear. Does she feel the electric current pulsing all around us?

I can't explain it. This instant attraction. This urge to claim her. To protect her. To make her mine. To go back in time and take back every mistake if it meant getting a do over with her.

This primal instinct to throw her down right here and claim her as mine in front of the club consumes my thoughts.

There was a time when she was all I ever wanted.

Desperate to make sense of the hectic and feral stream of emotions churning inside me, I keep stealing glances at her, wondering if she's a witch who's put a spell on me.

Does she have any idea how much I've missed her?

How deeply I crave her touch?

She will hardly look at me and it's killing me. There's so much that has been left unsaid between us. It's taking every ounce of strength I have not to give into these impulsive thoughts.

I ground myself by focusing on one thing in the room. The noise.

Classic rock hums through the sound system coupled with the noise of pool balls clacking against each other occupy her attention while the awkward silence stretching between us fills mine. The surrounding air is tense and heavy. Thick enough to cut with the blade of my pocket knife.

Henley strums along on his guitar, matching the chords to Hotel California as Darlene watches him dreamily, hoping he'll rail her tonight.

Twilah Jane and Kitty keep looking over at us from the bar. It's not like me to bring anyone to the clubhouse. At least not on display like this.

"Why am I here?" Lottie finally breaks the silence.

"To have a drink with me."

She shoots me an exasperated expression, lifting her brows. "Why am I really here?"

I'd be skeptical too if I were her. After the way I treated her back then. I should have handled her with more care. "I fucked up. Back then. You needed me and I wasn't there for you."

"We seriously do not have to talk about it."

I peel the corners of the label on my long neck. "I owe you an apology."

"For what?" She angles toward me. "Turning me down and hooking up with my best friend instead?"

"It wasn't like that."

"Ha." She slaps a palm down on the table in challenge. "It was exactly like that."

"What do you want me to say?"

"If this is your way of apologizing, you could use some work."

"All right. I'm sorry for being such an asshole. Becky had great tits, though."

"I hate you." She shoves against me.

"No, you don't."

"All men suck."

"Not all." I take a hard drink.

"Name me one good guy."

"Tyrant."

She snorts. "Yeah okay."

"I'm being serious. You should see him with his ol' lady and kid."

"He's a father?"

"Well, Gracie Joy is Blair's kid from the guy she was with. Her ex was a real piece of work." I dive into the story about Tyrant picking up Blair on his way to Vegas when she was hitchhiking and what crazy religious fanatics his group of followers were. Fucking cult.

"Hearing that." She shakes her head slightly. Her dark hair falls around her shoulders in silky waves I want to run my fingers through. "Cade doesn't sound too bad."

"Who the fuck is Cade?"

"Easy, killer. No one you need to concern yourself with."

"Did he fuck you over?"

"More like he ghosted me. I don't want to talk about it."

"I'm sorry."

"I'm used to it."

"You shouldn't be."

"Smooth. Too bad that shit doesn't work on me. You forget I know you and have watched you run game too many times."

"I'm not fucking with you or playing games. I wouldn't do that. Not with you."

"I may not have been present in your life these past ten years, but I guarantee you've not been a choirboy."

"Never claimed that."

"Just admit it. You're a total player."

"You think I'd fuck you over?"

"Why are we even talking about this? I don't even know why I'm here. I should go."

"You just got here. Stay." I squeeze her upper thigh. "How have you been? Ghosting douche bags aside. Of course."

She glances down at my possessive grip on her bare thigh and clears her throat. "Like I said. I should get home."

"Not so fast, beautiful." Loosening my grip on her thigh, I realize how uncomfortable she might be with my intimate touch. It's been ten years. I doubt she's still harboring a crush on me. Not after all these years. I finish my beer and signal Asphalt to bring me another round.

Lottie pulls back, creating too much distance between us for my liking. Her piercing blue eyes study me like she's reading her favorite book. "I see you're still hardheaded."

"No doubt." I grin as Asphalt replaces my empty bottle with a full one.

Mimicking my earlier action, she picks at the label on her own beer. "What do you really want, Seth?"

"Call me Creed when we're at the clubhouse."

"All right, Creed," her voice softens, and my road name rolls off her tongue, smooth as a good whiskey. "What do you want from me?"

"Why do I have to want something?"

"One, you're you. Two, you've not bothered to look me up all this time."

"Maybe I've missed you."

"Why? It doesn't look like you have a shortage of groupies."

"Careful. Almost sounds as if you're jealous."

"Learned that lesson once. I'm not looking to repeat past mistakes."

"What makes you think we'd be a mistake?"

She lets out a long huff. "Gee, Creed. I don't know. Want me to write you a list?" Her voice is laced with the bitterness of the memories she holds of the Becky situation and those that came before her. "Why would this time be any different for you than all the rest? Why would you treat me any differently than anyone else?"

"I'm older and wiser. People do change, Charlotte."

"Don't call me that. You sound like your father and it's too weird."

"Never compare me to that bastard."

"You know what I meant. Besides, you should know better than anyone that people never change. They simply get better at hiding their true nature. My mother had no idea your father was an alcoholic before it was nearly too late."

She's got me there, but she's wrong. We aren't our parents. I'm nothing like my old man. The tension between us pulls tight, like a wire about to snap. I've changed.

"I'm not my old man. I'd never be reckless with your heart."

She sputters, and nearly spits out her beer, getting choked. "Slow down and dial things back a notch."

"Look, you've got no reason to trust me. I've always lived in the moment and that's all I have ever offered in the past. I get that."

"You don't even know me. Sure, you knew the old me. The naïve girl with stars in her eyes who thought fairytales were real."

"I'd give you the fairytale if you'd let me."

"Just like that." She snaps her fingers. "You think it would be that easy? After all this time, I'm supposed to fall into your arms and swoon. Life doesn't work that way."

"I know I hurt you, but you weren't innocent in the shit that went down between us."

"I never fucked your friends, Creed."

Chapter Five

Lottie

"You really think that. Don't you? That I fucked that Becky bitch. Never touched her. Gave her a lift, and that was it. Didn't even walk her to her door. Hand to God if she told you anything different, then she lied."

I stare at Seth, wanting more than anything to believe him. He's right. I assumed. I stopped talking to Becky after that night. I withdrew from everyone, and no one cared enough to reach out. Not even him. He did what he's good at and disappeared.

"It's getting late. I work in the morning."

"I don't want you to go, Lottie." The way he says my name still influences me. The deep and throaty tone travels straight between my thighs.

Being here with him is dangerous. It's easy to forget that he broke my heart not once, but twice. All I wanted was to be his and now here we are years later. Nothing stands between us. But I can't allow myself to fall again. I can't go through losing him again. The last time, coupled with the loss of my mother, nearly killed me. I worked hard to claw myself out of that hole.

"I never should have come."

His brow crinkles. "Why did you?" The hurt in his voice isn't lost on me.

"Old habit." I shrug. "Curiosity."

"Alright, beautiful," he tells me, letting out a sigh that echoes with defeat. "Are you good to drive yourself?"

"Mhmm." I nod, avoiding the heartbreak evident in his eyes. Part of me wants him to beg me to stay. I know he won't. Creed isn't the type to beg. He's never had a problem letting me go or walking away. Tonight shouldn't be any different.

My hands tremble as I push up from my chair. I glance back at him one last time as he knocks back the rest of his beer. I offer him a faint smile and step into the chilly night air, sucking in a deep shuddering breath, begging myself not to cry.

I didn't think seeing him again would be this hard.

Not after all this time.

That's a lie.

I knew it would be, but I thought I'd at least be over the loss of him.

Now that I've breathed him in once more, the sting is just as bitter and harsh as it ever was.

The door slams shut behind me, muffling the music as I hurry toward my car, leaving Tonya here with Ghoul. They went off somewhere as soon as we arrived. I'll return her dress next time I see her at work.

I've gotta get out of here before I do something I'll regret.

Seth Creed once was my entire world. I tailored my entire existence around him and he's back like a ghost from the past. A reminder that I was never good enough for him or anyone. He didn't want me then. Why would he want me now?

Only once I'm in the privacy of my car do I allow the dam of emotions to break as tears stream down my face. I never thought of all people I'd bump into tonight that Seth would be one of them.

He's back and every bit as tempting and dangerous as he ever was.

Driving away from the clubhouse, from Creed, the road is as dark and empty as my hollow heart. Regret washes over me. An overwhelming sadness for all the things I didn't have the courage to say plague me. I grip the steering wheel so tightly my fingers ache as deeply as my soul.

After all this time, the chemistry between us is undeniable. My former stepbrother is everything I remember. A deadly combination of equal parts charming, handsome, and dangerous.

Lethal to my heart.

A man who makes me lose all control of my senses.

I keep seeing his devilish smirk throughout my drive.

Was he telling the truth about Becky?

Was he serious about missing me, or was he hoping to get laid?

Driving down my street, my apartment building coming into view is a comforting sight.

There's nothing better than the safety of home. My apartment is my sanctuary. I splurged on my bed and am still paying off the expensive mattress I purchased with one of those in-store credit cards. I deserve it. I work hard and a girl has to treat herself sometimes.

I wipe away my tears and grab my bag from work that has my clothes in it and juggle my shoes and keys. A shiver passes through me and that creepy sensation like I'm being watched captures my attention. I dash toward the building, cursing myself for never putting that bear spray on my key ring. I forgot to leave my outdoor light on, but thankfully the low glow of orange radiating from my neighbor's doorway across the hall is enough to illuminate my welcome mat.

Hurriedly, I unlock my door, dropping my work shoes in the process. Ugh. If I was in a horror movie, the killer would have captured me by now. I debate leaving my shoes where they lay, but knowing my luck, someone would steal them. My next investment should be one of those doorbell security cameras.

Once inside, I kick my shoes off and dump my belongings on one of the breakfast stools. I don't bother to switch any lights on. My apartment is a small one bedroom, one bathroom unit with an open kitchen and living room. I pad down to the short hallway to my bedroom and shimmy out of Tonya's dress. The smart choice would be to crawl into my bed and get some sleep, but with the way my thoughts are racing, I'll never be able to get comfortable. I slip into my pajamas and return to the kitchen and one of my worst habits.

Eating my feelings in the form of cookies and drowning my sorrows with milk. With every bite and swallow, I attempt to chase away thoughts of how Seth's hands felt on me and how his scent was all too familiar. Woodsy and smoky. The timber of his voice when he spoke my name. Deep and gravelly. Sexy. The way he looked at me like I was still his favorite girl. Like maybe he might love me still if he ever did.

I plop down in my oversized chair that takes up more than half of my living room and reach for the remote to my television. Since I'm not getting any sleep anytime soon, I may as well find something to watch to distract me from thinking about the past, but especially him. Flipping through the channels, I'm sensing a pattern. Romantic movies and shows seem to taunt me. A reality show titled A second Chance with my Ex. A Christmas commercial from a jewelry store when it's not even Halloween, with the tagline 'Every Kiss Begins with Kay.'

I roll my eyes and switch the tv off. Noise from the nearby freeway sounds particularly loud tonight. Even the sound of commercial trucks can't drown out my thoughts. Chill bumps fan along my arms, and I get up to turn my ceiling fan off, only to notice that it's not on.

I rub my arms, check the thermostat, then I look at my sliding glass door, noticing that it's slightly ajar. That's strange. I always keep it closed. I don't always lock it because I'm on the seventh floor and only a crazy person would try to climb the rickety fire escape. The building I live in is old as dirt, but the units have some modern updates with newer flooring and midlevel appliances.

We don't have security or anything like that, although this has always been a relatively safe place to live. I'm still creeped out by the idea of someone being here in my personal space, rifling through my things or worse. Waiting for me.

I close the door and lock it.

I know I'm being ridiculous, but I do a quick sweep of every room to make sure nothing is out of place. Surely if someone were in here with me, I'd spotted them when I changed clothes?

Nothing seems amiss in the kitchen outside of my milk and cookie mess on the counter, but the slithering sensation of unease bubbling in the pit of my stomach refuses to dissipate. My imagination is in overdrive. Morphing shadows into grotesque shapes on the walls and making every creak of the old building sound like a footstep.

I return to my room and go as far as checking under my bed and in my closet, growing increasingly irritated with my silly paranoia. This is why I don't watch scary movies. I get scared by them way too easily.

The last place left to check is my bathroom. It would be my luck that some psycho is hiding behind my shower curtain waiting to jump out and grab me like in some slasher flick. My hand trembles as I reach for the curtain and muster an ounce of dignity by not peeing my pants as I yank it back.

Empty, save my body wash and shampoo.

I laugh to myself as the adrenaline coursing through my veins wains.

Satisfied that I'm alone and merely delusional, I go to my bedroom and pull my crumpled sheets and blanket back. I just need to forget this whole day ever happened.

But I especially need to forget all about Seth Creed.

His dark eyes.

Rough hands.

Inked skin.

His image is conjured to life the moment I close my eyes.

All brutal and savage.

A rough and tumble biker whom I should avoid at any and all costs. That's what my brain tells me. My heart, however. My stupid, stupid heart still carries a torch for him that shines brighter than the brightest stars.

Rolling to my side, I stare out my bedroom window, wondering if he's still thinking of me. I slide an arm under my pillow and touch something cold and freeze. My pulse spikes as I wrap a fist around what feels like something small and metal.

Sitting up, I flick on the lamp on my nightstand, knocking the book I've been reading onto the floor with a heavy thud. I open my palm, discovering a single bullet. The reality that someone has invaded my home not only chills me to the bone, it terrifies me.

Is this a sick joke?

I turn the metal over between my fingers, noticing one side feels rougher than the rest.

There's an X etched there.

Bile churns in the pit of my stomach.

This isn't funny.

I feel violated.

Is whoever left this here watching me now?

I'm never getting any sleep tonight.

Sleep finally claimed me around four in the morning. Three hours before my shift was set to start. I never call in but today I'm taking the day off to buy security cameras that I can't afford but desperately need after last night.

I don't know what kind of game someone is trying to play with me, but I'm not taking any chances. I called management and asked to have my locks changed. I should have done it the second Cade skipped out on me. Would he have stuck the bullet under my pillow?

I don't know why he would do something so cruel and fucked up, but who else could it have been?

Seth had no idea I was even in the area, until last night, and he'd have no reason to screw with me. Not like this.

I'm seriously freaked out.

Before exiting my apartment, I check the peephole three times to make sure someone isn't waiting outside of my door. When I get to my car, I scan the parking lot for suspicious people and vehicles, then check my backseat and the trunk.

Calling the police would be useless. They have more important things to focus their efforts on. If I tell Seth, he'll go all macho on me, and I'm not sure if I'm prepared for that. He can be pretty intense without even trying.

I don't even get backed out of my parking space before my boss is calling me back and begging me to come in. Apparently, Cher called out right after I did. Both her boys have the flu. I'm too much of a people pleaser because I give in. I can get the security system after I get off, I suppose.

I glance down at my phone, at the new text from Tonya, wanting to know what I think of Ghouls' friend.

If she only knew his friend is Seth Creed, my former step brother I share a complicated past with.

I'll tell you later.

I send my response and grab the breakfast platters for table seven.

At least work has been a busy and welcomed distraction from the events of last night.

I manage to go through the motions, serving tables, re-filling coffee mugs, and flashing courteous smiles. Every so often, when my guard is down, my mind drifts back to Seth. His deep, growly voice echoes in my ears. His rough and possessive touch lingers on my skin. His woodsy and masculine scent... it's everywhere, as if he's here with me. I swear our new busser, Chris, must be wearing the same cologne as him or every man in this greasy joint is. If not, I've truly lost it and am smelling phantom scents.

That's the worst part of working here. Always smelling a deep fryer. It's damn hard to get the scent of grease out of my hair.

A burst of laughter from one table yanks me back to my existence outside of my thoughts. It's a group of college guys who are probably nursing their morning hangovers with black coffee and toast. I force a smile and head over to check on them.

"Can I get anyone a refill?"

One of them gets a bit ballsy and asks for my number. It's nothing I can't handle. I'm used to the forwardness of some of the flirtier truckers we get. I let him down gently and refill their coffees, hoping they will still leave a tip.

My mind drifts back to the bullet I found under my pillow and now every customer and every sound seems suspect and out of place. I'm jumpy and making avoidable mistakes like writing order downs wrong. Spilling drinks.

As soon as I get the chance, I slip into the kitchen for a breather. I lean against the cool stainless-steel counter, closing my eyes as I try to steady my racing thoughts. How did that bullet end up at my place? Was it a warning from Cade? Or was a stranger trying to send some sort of message? Did they get the wrong apartment? But why would someone want my neighbor dead? George is the sweetest man who always gives out full size candy to trick or treaters. He wouldn't hurt a fly.

The swinging kitchen doors creak open, and I sigh a breath of relief. It's only Chris, our server's assistant in training.

"Some dude is asking for you," he tells me.

A new intense surge of anxiety grips me, rooting me in place. The last thing I need is another surprise. I start to ask Chris what the guy looks like, but he's already back to work. I shake off the nerves and strut into the dining area like I don't have a care in the world. I'm taken aback when I see him.

What's he doing here and how did he know I'd be here?

Seth Creed"s in my section, kicking back in the booth, appearing totally relaxed like he does this all the time. His gorgeous green eyes that never fail to take my breath away are focused on me. A strange sense of calm washes over me as our gazes meet. Then he smiles that dimpled smile of his, and my heart skips a beat.

Slowly, I close the distance separating us, trying not to let his presence get to me. As I approach the table, he smiles wider.

"Hey, hellcat."

CHAPTER SIX

CREED

"Was that who I thought it was last night?" Rogue questions me as he lines up his stick for his next shot.

"If you're talking about Lottie, then yup."

"Damn. She's changed. Where has she been all these years?"

I cup the back of my neck. "Couldn't tell you. I haven't kept tabs."

He glances at me with lifted brows and wearing a smirk that says, 'yeah right' while taking his shot and sinking the eight ball to win the game.

"Seriously. Lost track of her when she was in college. Always figured she'd marry up and settle down with a couple of kids with some preppy fucker. Someone who could offer her more."

"More than you?"

"It's not like that."

"Bullshit. Always been the way of things between you. She was always chasing after you with hearts in her eyes, doing anything and everything to get your attention. Now it looks like the tables have turned."

I never told anyone about Lottie and me hooking up, but I guess we weren't as secretive as I thought back then.

"If I got that wrong, then maybe I'll hit her up. Take her out to dinner. Buy her a steak or some shit."

"The fuck you will." I snarl, and he bursts out laughing, doubling over, holding his stomach.

"You should see your face." He holds both palms up in surrender.

"Fuck you. Asshole."

He flips me off and picks up his empty bottle, motioning to Asphalt for another, since it's about the only drink he can be trusted to serve. Dumbass makes the weakest drinks on the planet. If he's behind the bar, no one is catching a buzz.

I fire up a joint to mellow myself out after Rogue's antics.

Truth is, I've been tempted to track her ass down many times through the years that's separated us, but I figured I was the last person she'd want to see. Last night, however, changes shit. That magnetic pull that always tethered us together is as strong as it ever was. If not, more so.

She can play hard to get all she wants, but we both know at the end of the day I'm the man she belongs to. She's always been mine. I just need to remind her.

"So, what are you going to do?" Tyrant asks.

"About what?"

"Lottie, the little hottie with a body." He chuckles as I glare at him.

"Shut up."

"I'm just saying, man. This could be your chance to have something good."

"You gonna make love to that joint or smoke it?" Ghoul asks, grabbing it from me.

"You're one to talk. Way you string that Tonya chick along every time you roll into town."

"I'm just looking for a good time. Nothing long term like you sad sacks of shit." He takes a hard toke and gets choked up on the intake of smoke.

"Right. Guess that's why you hit her up first thing every time you roll into town."

He shrugs. "She's a sure thing."

"So is Kitty." I remind him. Not that I need to.

"Whatever." He passes me the blunt.

I take a hit and ask out of curiosity. "What was the deal with that Rage fucker? Is Tonya his woman or something?"

"Dude is a fucking whacko. Get this. They were married for five years, and she finally gets pregnant and partway through the pregnancy they find out their baby has a disability. This asshole leaves her high and dry and claims there's no way the kid is his. That he'd never father a kid with special needs. Signed his rights away when she went after child support. Says the DNA test was rigged."

"Next time I see him, I'll kick his ass for free," I grumble. "Fuck that guy."

"Answer me something. How do you know Tonya's friend?"

"Long story."

Tyrant grins. "She's his stepsister."

"Former," I clarify.

"Hell, that explains a lot," Ghouls says.

"What's that supposed to mean?"

"Your type. Nearly every bitch you get all into looks like her."

"No, they don't." I snuff the bud out and fold my arms across my chest.

"Did I ruffle your feathers, bro?" he chuckles. "Think about it. You've been hung up on that girl from West Virginia. She's like a carbon copy of Lottie. Dark hair. Blue eyes. Banging curves. Tell me I'm wrong."

I'd like to prove him wrong and pull up Ember's social media profile to show him, but looking at her picture, there's no denying it. I have a type. Lottie. I've spent the past ten years looking for her in every woman I've been with. Chasing the ghost of her. Trying to find what I lost.

She was the first and only girl I've ever loved. We were both young and made mistakes, me most of all.

Shit. I've gotta prove to her that this time around, I'm going to do things right.

Show her I'm not some loser that can't provide for her. I make damn good money doing what I do. I can give her the good life I promised. I shoot off a text to our contractor asking what it'd take to finish my build before Halloween. I need my own place. I sure as fuck don't want to bring Lottie back here, where everyone will be watching us like their favorite reality show now that everyone has heard our shared history.

"Breaking news," the reporter's voice blares from the tv by the bar. "A jogger who was found dead in the park has been identified. Local businessman Lonnie Kovack was an avid jogger, and authorities have ruled his death an accident. Officials say his family is devastated and want to remind everyone about taking proper safety precautions. They say what happened to Lonnie was a freak accident. It is believed he tripped on wet leaves and hit his head on a rock, of all things."

I grab the remote off the bar and switch the channel.

Minutes later, I receive an email that a new deposit is available in my account. A bonus for a job well done, no doubt. Good. I'm going to need it to pay for the construction of my place. The guy I hired is good, but he's not cheap. This is going to cost me a whack.

Getting to take Lottie there when I win her back will be worth any price.

Speaking of Lottie, I'm interested in knowing who this Cade bastard is that she was dating.

It hits me that I know nothing about her now. Not where she works or what she does for a living. No clue where she even lives. However, I know what she drives.

With a little poking around, I'll have her address and place of employment within an hour. Then I'll figure out who this Cade fuck is.

I head to my room here at the clubhouse and fire up my laptop. I type in her name when I receive an email notification with the subject line: your stepsister is in trouble. Which only means one thing. I've got another job to do. It's a stupid code I chose off the list of options.

I've barely reconnected with Lottie and already I've gotta ride out. I don't want to, but the money is too good to pass up.

I grab my backpack from my closet and shove some clean clothes inside and my burner phone. My latest piece with the serial number etched off goes between my shirts. I'll stop at Wyatt's to gas up and grab a few snacks for my trip. I'm not sure how long I'll be gone. Won't know the job until Merc gives me my orders. He owns the Velvet Rooster. A shithole bar in the middle of nowhere is his cover. Old fuck has his fingers in several pies. He can make anyone disappear. Hell, I've seen him bring gangsters back from the dead and turn them into bikers. Men like Ghost who was once in line to be a Capo. Now, years after his supposed death, he's the Prez of Black Rebel Riders' MC Chicago chapter. Married him, a pretty little princess named Adeline. Last I heard, she's pregnant. And good for him. After the shit that happened to him. His pregnant bride to be and his father were gunned down on the church steps on his wedding day. If anyone deserves something good, it is that man.

It gives me hope that I'll get another chance with Lottie. Fuck. I'm not leaving it to chance. I'm not giving her a choice this time around.

I go in search of Prez to let him know I'm hitting the road.

"I've got a meeting."

"So soon?" His eyes crinkle around the edges, showing a hint of concern.

I don't normally do back-to-back jobs, but it's also not unusual in this business.

"Unfortunately."

I find Zero, one of the prospects. "Do me a solid. Look up an old friend of mine and send me everything you can find on her. Lottie Rae Pierce. Write that shit down and send it to me while I'm on the road."

"I'm on it."

I would ask Country to look after her, but hell, he'd probably sweep her off her feet. If anyone could take her from me, it'd be that bastard and his monster dick.

"Thanks, man.

"Check in when you can," Prez calls out after me.

I catch Ghoul in the parking lot, about to take Tonya home.

"Where can I find your friend?"

"Lottie?"

I run a hand over my hair. "Yeah."

I watch as Lottie struts toward me in her tight black pants, her ponytail swinging in time with the sway of her hips. She's mesmerizing and hypnotizing every motherfucker in the joint and doesn't even know it.

No wonder I had to wait twenty minutes for a table to free up in her section. Every man in here is staring at her ass. Who can blame them? She's got a damn fine ass.

"Hey, hellcat?" I flash a grin at her, and she scowls.

"What are you doing here?"

"A man needs to eat."

"There are other restaurants you can go to."

"Not any with an ass as fine as yours."

She rolls her eyes, but I don't miss the hint of pink coloring her cheeks.

"What do you want, Seth? You want breakfast? Here's your menu." She slams it onto the table.

But it's not the food I hunger for. I study her reactions carefully, calculating how much further I can push her.

I watch her take a deep breath, steeling her spine before she speaks again.

"Seth, I'm working. What do you want?"

I shrug nonchalantly. "Some breakfast... and maybe a little conversation. Is that too much to ask?"

"Yes," she retorts immediately, but her gaze betrays her. Her eyes flicker towards the empty seat across from me before she can stop herself.

"Sit with me," I demand, not missing the opportunity to spend even a few minutes with her before I have to leave town. Her eyebrows shoot up in disbelief, but there's a hint of curiosity with the way her lips twitch like she wants to smile.

"No way. I can't," she protests, but there isn't any genuine conviction behind her words.

"Why not?"

"Because this is my job, and I have customers to serve."

I glance around, noting the now mostly empty tables around us. The morning rush appears to be over.

"I'm sure they can survive without their waitress for a few minutes. Humor me."

A busboy emerges from the kitchen to clear the surrounding abandoned tables. He looks at us, confusion apparent. His brows drawing deeper together as she plops into the seat.

Maybe he has a crush on her and isn't used to seeing her with someone.

I watch him grab the crumpled bills off the tables. Wordlessly, he hands the bills over to Lottie, then returns to the back, giving us some privacy.

"It's good to see you again."

"Cut the crap and tell me what you're really doing here."

"You kept it."

She fingers the locket hanging around her neck. The one I gave her on her sixteenth birthday.

"So what? It's pretty."

"Nothing." I let it go.

"What do you want to eat?" she pulls an order pad from the pocket of her apron and clicks her pen open.

"Why don't you surprise me?"

She drops the pen and crosses her arms defensively over her chest. "This is some sort of game to you, isn't it?"

"There's no game being played here," I respond quickly, irritated that she thinks I would purposely fuck with her. "I've got to head out of town for a bit. Wanted to see you before I go. That's all."

"Hmm." She studies me a beat and the chime for the front door sounds. "I've gotta get back to it. I'll put your order in." She slides out of the booth.

As she turns to leave, I reach out and gently grab her wrist, halting her in her tracks. "Lottie. When I get back to town, let me take you to dinner."

"I don't…"

"Think about it, beautiful."

She nods and puts my order in with the kitchen. She gets back to work as her tables fill back up with the lunch rush.

Now and then, she throws me quick glances, her eyes showing a mix of confusion, mistrust, and curiosity. I can see she's trying to figure out if she wants to waste her time with me. I can't blame her for doubting me. Our past is littered with secrets and half-truths. Betrayals that cut from both ends. Neither of us are innocent parties in the way we began or how we ended.

I watch her float between tables, chatting with customers, refilling coffee mugs and grabbing takeout orders from the kitchen window for customers waiting at the counter. Fuck me. I've missed her. Missed this sassy and gorgeous hellcat who can put a man in his place without batting an eyelash.

She's beautiful.

I'm going to make her mine again.

After what feels like an eternity, she finally returns to my table with a plate overflowing with scrambled eggs, crispy bacon, hash browns, and toast. The perfect choice to fill me up before I head out. Saves me from grabbing a bunch of junky snacks from the gas station that will only make me tired and moody.

"Enjoy," she says curtly before walking away again, saving her pleasantries for her other tables. I don't mind the attitude. Sparring with Lottie has always turned me on.

Digging into my meal gives me something to do besides watch her every move and overthinking everything that's happening between us. Of course, over the years I've tried to forget her, but there's always been a void that can only be filled by her.

After her mom passed, I never thought I'd see her again, but now she's here. Living a town over from me. It's got to be fate or some bullshit like that.

I walked away before. Ran is more like it. Not this time around.

As I finish my plate, I steal glances at her once again. She's back to her tables, her ponytail bobbing with each hurried step she takes as she rushes to make sure everyone has what they need.

I should pay my tab and leave her to it, but I can't. Not until she agrees to dinner or at least gives me her number. Not that I can't find it easy enough. There's not many people named Charlotte Rae Pierce in the area that's the same age as her.

I decide to wait for the rush to subside before bringing up dinner once more. Maybe Lottie wants nothing to do with me. Maybe she's moved on, but my heart still beats for her. Even after all these years. I know what I've been missing and what I want.

Her.

Always Lottie.

When the crowd thins once more, she appears by my table again, a forced smile on her face.

"Can I get you anything else?"

"Your number."

Her smile wavers at that. She glances around nervously.

"I don't have time for this," she hisses. "I have work to do."

"Make time," I insist, looking directly into her eyes.

"God. You're so stubborn."

"Digits, babe. Write'm down."

"Ugh." She complains but does as she's told. She writes her number on a ticket and rips it off the pad.

"Better not be a fake."

"Guess you'll have to trust me."

"Right." I pay my tab and get on the road.

Chapter Seven

Lottie

"Was that dude your boyfriend or something?" Chris asks from the back exit where he's hanging his head out the door to take a quick smoke break.

"An old friend," I volunteer. Not that it's any of his business.

"Is he aware he's only a friend?"

"I'm not sure what you mean. What's it to you, anyway?"

"I didn't mean to offend you. My bad."

"Well, you didn't," I mutter and scan the schedule.

I don't work the same shift with Tonya again for a few days. Bummer. Looks like I share nearly all my shifts with the new busboy. I miss our old one. Jeremy was great. He didn't ask too many questions and never stole anyone's tips. But he ran off and joined the Army and was shipped off for basics back in August. We've gone through at least four others since then.

I grab my stuff and book it to my car, happy my shift has ended.

I make the drive home mindlessly. Once inside, I do my usual routine of stripping off my work gear and doom scrolling the internet for a bit. Seth's profile isn't too hard to find, though he doesn't appear to be very active. At least not publicly. His work isn't listed. I can't see his friends.

I debate on sending a friend request but decide against it. The last thing I need to do is encourage him, but I'd be a liar if I said I'm not curious.

If I'm being honest with myself, I've missed him and part of me has always wondered what happened to him. I toy with the locket hanging around my neck. I've always worn it out of habit. At least that's what I've always told myself. I guess I couldn't bring myself to part with my last reminder of him.

I don't want to stay here in my apartment where I'm going to sit alone and be paranoid that someone is going to break in and hack my body into teeny pieces and shove them in a suitcase and toss me in a river or something.

I take a quick shower to get the grime off of me from work, then head over to Tonya's to listen to her gab about her night with Ghoul and bitch about her ex. Her problems and love life will be a great distraction from overthinking mine.

Going through the same ritual as this morning, I check my fire escape and look out the peephole. Outside, once again I scan for unfamiliar cars and faces, then check my backseat and trunk. That bullet under my pillow has creeped me the hell out. On the drive to Tonya's, I'm constantly checking my mirrors to see if anyone is following me.

If I didn't have the bullet as proof, I'd believe I dreamed the whole thing. Thankfully, work kept me busy enough that it wasn't constantly on my mind. Seeing Seth was a welcome distraction, even if ninety percent of the time he was working his way under my skin.

I hit the drive-thru of a local pizza place and pick up a ready-made pepperoni and an order of these cheese stuffed muffin thingies that Kaydence loves. Tonya will forgive me for blowing off her texts from earlier when I show up with dinner, saving her from having to cook.

The second she opens her door to see me holding the food, I'm rewarded with her infectious smile. Despite the shitty hand life has dealt her, she always finds the bright side of any situation. That's one of the things I admire most about her.

"Just in time. If I had to make macaroni and nuggets one more time this week, I was going to lose my mind."

"There could be worse things. When I was a kid, I only wanted grilled cheese sandwiches dipped in ketchup."

She scrunches her nose up. "Ew. You are nasty."

"Ha. Says the weirdo who dips a cinnamon bun in her chili."

"It's okay to be wrong."

"You know what? I think I'll take my pizza and go home."

"Girl, get your ass in here and hush."

"That's what I thought." I breeze past her as she stands aside for me to enter. If my hands weren't full, I'd flip my hair. I dump my offerings at the kitchen table. Kaydence tugs on my hand, then holds her arms up, wanting me to hold her. I know what she wants. She loves jewelry and always wants to look at the locket I wear. As soon as I heft her onto my hip, she wraps her fingers around the silver heart. "Do you want some pizza puffs?"

Her face lights up and I untangle her fingers from the stranglehold she has on my necklace before plopping her bottom onto a chair. Tonya is already setting up her plate and cutting the pizza bites into four pieces, so they are easier for her to eat.

I grab a couple of paper plates and set us up with two slices of pizza each, then grab us both bottled water.

"You keep doing sweet stuff and I may have to give up on men and marry you instead," she teases.

"No offense, but you're not my type."

"Ouch."

"I don't want to take a punch from that Rage guy." I laugh, but I am only half joking. That due was unhinged.

"Ha. Funny."

"That was something." I sit next to Kaydence in case she needs any help to give Tonya a break so she can eat without interruption. Like most children, she wants to be considered a big kid who can do things on their own. She has a stubborn streak and can be prone to some tantrums when she doesn't get her way. Tonya is an exceptional mother, but I know it wears on her when she's had a string of bad days. I'm sure the stunt her ex pulled didn't help her stress levels.

She blows on her first slice, then takes a healthy bite. "Can you believe that?" she mumbles as she chews and shakes her head.

"I'm sure you have other things you're dying to talk about."

"After I get Kaydence a bath and to bed. Tell me about you and Creed. Seemed like the two of you knew each other."

The main reason I came over was to avoid all things Seth Creed, but should have known she'd be curious. "You wouldn't believe me if I told you."

"Try me."

"Uh." Kaydence grunts, unable to reach her sippy cup. I scoot it closer and allow her to grab the cup herself, which seems to appease her.

"As you were saying," Tonya presses. I know she will not let this go.

Simple is better. "We grew up together."

"Don't hold back. Spill the tea."

"There's not much to say. We lost contact and last night was the first time I've seen him in ten years or so."

"You dated."

"I'm not sure you could call it that. We fooled around. It's not a big deal."

"I thought we were friends."

"We are."

"So why are you giving me a careful answer?"

"It's complicated."

"Do you think I'm going to judge you or something? I tell you everything, Lottie. The good and the bad, because that's what friends do."

"You're right. I've got a lot on my mind. If I tell you something, you've got to promise me it stays between us."

"I'm a safe space."

"I know." I grab the pack of wipes that sit in the center of the table that Tonya keeps on hand for Kaydence and give the little cutie one before she smears pizza sauce all over my jeans. "It's not you. I'm scared," I admit.

"Let me set her up with a cartoon and we can talk on the balcony while I smoke."

While she gets Kaydence settled in her fenced in play area of the living room, I clean up the remnants of our meal.

Out on the balcony that shoots off the living room with Kaydence in full view through the sliding glass door, Tonya lights up a joint and offers me a hit.

"No, but thank you."

"Suit yourself." She takes a deep toke. "Now tell me about you and Creed."

"Our parents were married for a few years, and I wanted to be anywhere he was. I wanted to be with him. Be his. For a while I was. In secret. It ended badly because of miscommunications on both our parts and there really isn't much more to tell."

"Forbidden. I've gotta share this with my book group."

"What?"

"I won't tell them your name and I can post anonymously. Trust me, they will eat this shit up."

"Tonya. No way."

"Come on. Let us live through you. I want details. Are you still into him? You are, aren't you?"

"I don't know. Maybe, but we weren't good for each other."

"He's fucking hot."

"Looks aren't everything."

"No, but they sure as shit don't hurt." She takes another hit off her joint.

"Enough about me. What's up with you and Ghoul?"

"Remember. We listen and we don't judge," she cautions. "I know you don't like him, but he's sweet with me and we're having a good time. That's what I need. He allows me to gush about my spicy books and even tries out some of my favorite scenes. Last night, he brought in another dude."

I do my best to mask my surprised reaction.

"We get to the room he stays at when he's in town and this guy, I don't recall his name. I think he's one of the prospects or something is already waiting. I watched the two of them go at it. Making out. It was hot as fuck. Me and this other guy went down on Ghoul together while he was eating me. I was sitting on his face and the dude was down between his legs. I've never experienced anything like it. The whole thing was crazy and erotic. Filthy. Ghoul shot his load, and the guy spit it into my mouth. Then Ghoul fucked me while the guy fucked him. Ten out of ten would do it again."

"Wow. That was certainly descriptive. Sharing is not my thing, but hey whatever floats your boat."

"You're judging."

"No." I flash my palms upward. "I just wasn't expecting so many intimate details, and I can't help but wonder if Creed ever takes part."

"That was the first time he brought in another guy. We've done it with other girls, but I don't think Creed knows Ghoul is bisexual. I don't think he walks around advertising it based on the conversations we've had. Though he'd nut in his pants if you agreed to join us sometime."

"I'm flattered but I don't...yeah nope. Not going to happen. I love you, but I don't want to have sex with Ghoul or you or any other woman."

"You ever change your mind...I'm just saying you're hot and I'd be down."

"Let's talk about something else. I didn't tell you what's really got me freaking the fuck out."

"Hold that thought. Let me get Kaydence down."

"No worries. I should probably get home."

"I made shit weird, didn't I?"

"A little, but it's fine. I'll forget all about it in a day or five." I laugh.

"I like don't think about you naked or anything. It's just that you're my friend and I know you'd never fuck me over. And well, if you were curious. You'd be safe with me. You know?"

"I get it. We'll talk later. Okay?"

"You're not mad at me?"

"No. A little weirded out but also flattered."

"If you talk to your stepbrother or whatever, don't mention what I shared, yeah?"

"I'll take it to the grave." I make the sign of crossing my heart.

Leaving Tonya's, a familiar icy chill spreads down my spine. The creepy sensation of being watched overwhelms me as I climb into the driver's seat. I planned to stay at Tonya's longer, but the conversation grew strange and was going in a direction I shudder to think about. I don't judge. Whatever consenting adults choose to do is none of my business. I can't imagine Seth participating in a scenario like that. However, I don't know the man he is today or what he's been doing for the past ten years.

As I drive, I wonder if he's going to call. It would serve him right if I had given him a fake number, but I'm curious about him and if our flame still burns as brightly as it once did.

By the time I arrive home, I remember that I never went shopping.

I got too invested in being in my head to think about it. Until now.

Will someone be waiting for me?

Did they return while I was at work?

Did they get the wrong apartment?

Does the X mean what I think it means?

I need answers and no clue where to begin searching for them.

Chapter Eight

CREED

I pull up outside of the Velvet Rooster, dreading walking through the door. One never knows who they may have a run in with. One rule here is that no one spills blood at Merc's bar. Everyone here is in the business of killing or disappearing. It can be a competitive business at times. Not that there's any shortage of people who want someone dead or fuckers who deserve to die or people seeking a new life. There's been times in my life where I thought maybe that's what I needed. That's how I got into the killing game.

Found myself in a low place of chasing the high of the next fight and easy pussy. The purses I was winning weren't anything to brag about. Merc saw something in me others didn't. Hunger. Drive. He offered me something that was a high unlike anything I'd ever experienced. I tell myself that I could walk away anytime I want to, but I don't know if I can give up the thrill.

One glance around the parking lot and I recognize a familiar motorcycle. Belongs to a former nomad for what was the Royal Bastards MC out of Charleston, West Virginia. Guy who goes by the name Static. His brother Holy is the club's chaplain. The two of them are like daylight and dark. Two sides of the same coin. Like me, Static is a killer for hire. I was under the impression he got out when he hooked up with Rosie.

The tension I was experiencing rolls off my shoulders as they drop. As much as I love my life in Alabama, there's a part of me that misses my time spent at Devil's Playground in WV. There was a time I thought about patching over. The possibility of having Lottie back in my life solidifies that I made the right choice for me. I may have lost Ember to Smoke, but in the end, she wasn't the one for me. She's not Lottie.

Inside, I spot Static sitting at the bar nursing a beer and munching on the complimentary peanuts that I personally find stale. To each their own, though. He shoots me a chin lift and I drop onto the neighboring stool.

"Haven't seen your ugly mug in a while."

"Been busy. You know how it is. How's everyone doing these days?"

"Dust is settling after all the shit that went down."

"I hear that."

One of Merc's girls, Birdie, flips a coaster over in front of me on the bar and serves me a beer and moves back to the other end of the bar to pretend she's not listening to our conversation. The old man trained her well.

"Thought you retired?"

"Me too, but I've got a teen daughter, a woman, a mortgage and car payments. So here I am. What about you? Still kicking ass and taking names?"

"You know it." I take a hard pull from my beer and wait for my marching orders.

The road can be just as lonely as it is freeing. I pulled over for the night at what I refer to as a roachtel. And yes, it's exactly what it sounds like. A hole in the wall place that still accepts cash and rents rooms by the hour. Not a place you spend any real time at. No use in wasting money for a full night when what I want most is somewhere to close my eyes for a couple of hours that doesn't involve my ass worrying about getting arrested for trespassing or someone trying to rob me.

I don't bother kicking my shoes off and spread a plastic tarp on the bed. No way in hell do I want to lay my ass on the filthy blanket. I read somewhere once that motels and hotels alike rarely wash their comforters and the real lazy fucks won't even swap out the sheets unless they look gross.

I pull out my cell and lay my head at the foot of the bed away from the wall where the bedbugs are more likely to live. My skin crawls merely thinking about it. I fire off a text to the number Lottie gave me.

> You awake, hellcat?

...

Typing dots move, then stop.

I'm awaiting a 'you've got the wrong number' response when nothing happens.

> Don't leave me hanging.

...

More dots, but this time she replies.

I'm awake. Are you still out of town for work?

> Why? You missing me already?

Ha. You wish.

> Don't I, though. You thought anymore about dinner?

Maybe.

> It's not a no.

It's not a yes either.

But you're thinking about me.

I'm deciding where I want you to take me.

Anywhere you want. Name it.

Can we call?

She doesn't wait for me to answer before I'm getting a Facetime request.

"Hey beautiful." I greet her gorgeous baby blues filling my screen, but immediately I can tell something is wrong. She's wearing that timid expression she always wore right when I was about to get grounded because she tattled on me for something, and she was scared I was going to be pissed at her. I usually was. "What's wrong?"

"What makes you think there's anything wrong?"

"I know that look. What happened? You go tell my old man that I've been smoking reefer," I tease.

"That wasn't me."

"Bullshit."

"I was twelve and there was one of those Dare programs that week at school. I signed a pledge."

"Fucking fruitcake."

"What?"

"Nothing. Tell me the truth. What's got you twisted in knots?"

"Are you on a tarp?"

"This motel is scuzzy and don't change the subject."

She bites her bottom lip while tucking her dark hair behind her ears and wiggling to get more comfortable in the oversized chair she's seated in and moves on from her lip to chewing on her thumbnail. "Do you...um do you share partners with Ghoul?"

"Did that asshole say something to you?"

"Not exactly."

"I've been with two women at the same time, if that's what you're asking. Did Tonya say something? I've never fucked her or been in the same room when her and Ghoul are doing whatever they do." Lottie appears to visibly relax at my words. "I'd never share you with anyone, hellcat. Want you all to myself. But where is this shit coming from?"

"Only curious."

I don't doubt for one second there's something she's not telling me. Something her friend has said or did had to have provoked the question.

"Have you ever had a threesome?"

"What?"

"You asked me. Turnabout is fair play, babe."

"Hmm." Her mouth stretches wide as her arms go up over her head and she lets out a soft yawn. "I think I'm going to get ready for bed now."

"All right. I'll let you go. Sweet dreams, beautiful."

"Seth," she whispers my name. "I agree to dinner."

80

"It's a date." The call drops off, and I close my eyes with a smile.

"That's it, baby. Yeah. Shake it." Gino, my target, tosses bills at the stage. I've spent all day following this stupid fuck all over town.

I watch the stripper as she tugs at the strings of her G-string, snapping the thin material against her hips, teasing like she may accidentally flash us her beat up pussy. I thought the motel I'm staying at was a shithole until I entered this joint. Smells like piss, desperation, and body odor.

This bitch has track marks on her arms and one too many lip injections. I can't tell what's bigger. Her mouth or her fake tits.

This whole scene is fucking sad.

Gino is a sex addict who has trouble getting it up and owes the Cornbread Mafia more than his pathetic life is worth. They've ordered the hit, but it can't be in the family because he married into it through a cousin or something. For whatever reason, they hired me to off the greaseball.

I don't really care. I want to get this over with so I can get home to take Lottie out.

The performance gets worse when she spins around to show off her flabby ass and the lighting in here only seems to highlight her worst features. I don't feel sorry for her. She's Gino's whore that he pimps out on the side to fund both of their drug habits. The cunt has three kids with him, all given up for adoption. It's the only smart choice she's made. Too bad for her. She got in so deep with the wrong man. She signed her own death warrant the moment she first time she didn't walk away. Now the organization thinks she knows too much thanks to Loose Lips McGee, who has shared too much about the business.

I never thought I'd be here myself. Killing for profit. Having pity on a mark. I've never turned down a job before, but I'm conflicted. Would this bitch be a better person if she had a fresh start and was clean? Could she one day make it up to her children? The thought weighs heavily on me. At the end of the day, we all have choices and time after time, this cunt has proven that she loves her demons more than she loves herself.

I elbow Gino in the ribs. "She sure can move."

He looks me over, deciding if I'm a threat. I pretend to drunkenly pull out my huge wad of cash, dropping a few bills on the floor and throwing a few fifties and twenties at the whore.

"Hey man." He leans in close. "She likes to party. Know what I mean?" he arches his brows, wiggling them.

The idea of touching his skank has the bile in the pit of my stomach churning. Acid hits the back of my throat. "I've got a room if you think she'd be down."

"She'll do anything, and I do mean anything, for the right price."

I continue to play my part of the sloppy drunk who barely knows his own name and lure them back to the motel down the street. The room I checked into under a false name and paid for with cash for a week.

The bitch wastes no time drinking the beer I had waiting in the mini fridge. Gino gets right to it, pulling his flaccid cock out to stroke himself as his whore dances around the room. I watch from the doorway of the bathroom.

Her fake ass tits barely move. Her dark eyeliner is smudged beneath her eyes, giving her the racoon look. Fuck, this is sad and downright embarrassing.

"Don't tell me you're shy?" she shimmies her way over to me and takes my hands, trying to get me to dance with her. I laugh it off, but I'm about three seconds away from snapping her neck.

"Thought you like to party?" I take out a preloaded syringe filled with a cocktail that will make her go lights out permanently.

"I love to party," she coos. "Don't I, Gino."

"That's right, sugar. Nobody loves it more." The short, fat bastard pops a boner pill while continuing to stroke his worm of a dick. "I like to watch."

"Me too," I tell him with a wink that startles him. "Come on, sweetheart. Ladies first." I whip off my belt for a tourniquet and shove her down on the edge of the bed. "You too, big boy." I point a second syringe at my primary target. He shuffles out of the chair with his pants and underwear around his ankles and over to the bed next to his bitch as she tries to undo my jeans. "Not yet." I press my lips to hers, about to vomit from touching her.

"What about you?" Gino questions as his woman tightens the belt around his arm.

I press the plunger down. "I don't put poison in my veins." His eyes widen and he falls back on the bed, experiencing a temporary euphoria as the drugs burn through his veins.

"Do me," the soon to be dead chick begs, jerking the belt off Gino's arm.

"Sure thing."

Once they both pass out, I wipe down the room and paraphernalia. I put my belt back on and leave the scene, sticking a do not disturb sign on the door. As I'm climbing on my bike, my cell vibrates with a call from Lottie. I look at the time. It's three in the morning.

"Hellcat," I greet, unable to fight my smile.

"Seth," she cries. "I need you." The panic in her voice gives me pause as chills spread across the back of my neck and fan down my spine.

"What's wrong?"

"Please come as soon as you can. I think. I think I killed him."

CHAPTER NINE

Lottie

I didn't think the customers would ever stop coming tonight at work. I prefer to work the breakfast crowd over the dinner rush. In the morning people are generally in a better mood and happy to be getting a coffee. In the evening, I find customers are tired from work and rude. I stuff my tips in my bag and let my hair down. As I'm running my fingers through my hair to undo the tangles, Chris hesitates at the back door with the last bag of garbage of the night.

"Are you single?"

"What?" I laugh under my breath, taken aback.

"You said that guy the other day was just a friend, and I haven't noticed anyone else coming around."

"Are you?" I purse my lips, trying not to hurt his feelings. "Are you asking me out?"

"That depends on the answer to my question."

Oh no. Not only is he not my type, but now working with him is going to be even more awkward than it was already beginning to feel. "I don't date people I work with."

"I'll quit then." He has this hopeful and eager tone in his voice.

"I wouldn't and couldn't ask you to do that. You don't even know if you like me, and I just had a terrible breakup. I'm not really looking to date anyone at the moment, ya know?"

"I get it." he slinks out the door to take out the trash and I decide to leave out the front. I'm not saying he'd try something, but the guy gives off weird as hell vibes. It's like he's always watching me too closely. I can feel his gaze tracking me through the diner when I'm waiting on tables.

Walking to my car, I check over my shoulder to make sure he's not following me. As I'm crossing the street, I spot a car that looks similar to my ex-boyfriend's. My suspicion is confirmed when he pops out of the driver's side and ambushes me.

"Can we talk?"

"Have you been sneaking into my apartment?"

"Shit. Fuck." He wipes a hand over his sandy brown hair and cups the back of his neck. "No. Why? What happened?"

"Forget it. What do you want?"

"I really need to talk to you."

"About?"

"Us." He takes a step toward me, practically pressing me into the door of my car.

I laugh in his face. "There's not been an us since you ghosted me. So no, Cade. We can't talk about us. You've got some nerve."

"Let me explain." He stares at his feet. "I — Lottie. Please."

"Well. Say what you came to say. Spit it out already."

"Can we go somewhere?" He glances around like he's looking for someone. As if he's being watched.

"What the hell is going on?"

"I've wanted to reach out. I'm sorry. Things weren't supposed to go down like they did."

"Cool. We done?"

"It's not safe, Lottie."

"What do you mean?"

"Everything okay over there?" Chris calls out from across the street.

"I've gotta go." Cade turns and sprints back toward his car.

"Wait. Ugh." I stomp my foot as he speeds off.

Chris crosses the street as I'm getting in my car, and I don't have the spoons to be friendly right now. "I'm sorry. It looked like that guy was bothering you."

"He wasn't," I snap and practically slam the door in his face. I drive off and glance in my rearview mirror to see Chris staring after me, hands tucked in his pockets. I shouldn't have yelled at him, but it wasn't any of his business.

Even though I doubt he'd go home, I cruise past Cade's apartment. I don't see his car, but it looks like one of his lights is on. What did he mean? It's not safe? Is he in some kind of trouble? And if he is, why am I inviting myself to partake in his issues? Whatever they are, I should forget it and go home. I can't help but wonder if the bullet under my pillow was meant for him instead.

Where has he been all this time?

I have so many questions.

Against my better judgement, I park my car on the side street.

I've always hated Cade's apartment. It's why he practically lived with me. It's always given me the creeps. We had good times, though. We'd watch the people coming in and out of the dry cleaner's shop below and make up stories about what they were dropping off and why. There was one guy who seemed to be a regular. Cade always swore he worked for the mob. I brush off those thoughts because as many good times as we had, there were bad ones to outweigh them. I trudge up the dimly lit stairwell, debating turning back to my car, only I've already come this far. May as well get this over with.

There are only two apartments. One belonged to Cade and the one on the other side belonged to Mr. Honeycutt, a retired veteran who passed away about three months ago. No one ever moved into his unit, as far as I can tell.

I knock on Cade's door three times with no answer. I'm betting his spare key is still on the upper ledge of the doorframe. I'm not sure if I'm tall enough to reach it, but maybe the keypad on Mr. Honeycutt's door is the same as it was before. Cade had given it to me once to feed the cat when his neighbor was in the hospital. He also had a spare key to Cade's place. I knock on the other door a few times and hope that I'm not about to break into some poor stranger's place while they are in the shower or something. I punch in the code and bingo. Success. I grab the key and let myself in. The apartment is empty except for a stepladder and some remodeling stuff. Someone's been painting the walls. I borrow the stepladder and use it to check for Cade's key. Right where it always was. I hurry to unlock his door in case someone shows up.

Cade's place resembles the unit next door. Empty. Still, I do a quick walkthrough and check the bedroom closet. I don't know what I'm hoping to find. Nothing is here.

I have no choice other than to go home. I'm not wasting my night driving around searching for him. So that's exactly what I do. Maybe he's screwing with me. Maybe he gets off on freaking people out. Whatever this game is, I'm not taking part. I refuse.

At home, I shut my car off and out of habit I look around. I don't see anything or anyone out of place and hate that I have this sense of urgency to check every single time I'm coming or going.

My phone vibrates with a text from an unknown number.

I slide my thumb across the screen and click the messages. There's only one word.

Sorry.

Fuck off, Cade.

I block the number after I hit send.

Tomorrow I'm going to the animal shelter and adopting the biggest and meanest dog they have, and I'll train him or her to bite the ass off anyone who enters my apartment uninvited. No matter who they are.

As soon as I hit the breezeway, the atmosphere feels off. The hair on my arms stands at attention, and that uneasy sensation of being watched consumes me. I consider knocking on my neighbor's door and asking them to walk into my place with me. A sane person would call the police and have them enter first. I don't want to be afraid of my apartment. This has to stop. I've let Cade and his little tricks psyche me out.

I take one more glance back at the parking lot. I'm being dumb. I've got a frozen ready to be baked pot pie waiting in the freezer for me and a new tub of cookies n' cream ice cream. While my dinner bakes, I'm taking a bubble bath and forgetting all about threats, bullets, games, and Cade.

Sucking a deep breath, I exhale and get over my paranoia by unlocking the door. Creeping through the doorway quietly, I pause and listen for any unusual noises, then check the sliding door that leads to the fire escape. Locked as it should be. I flip on all the lights, set the oven to preheat, lay out my pajamas, and run my bathwater. My food takes forty-five minutes to bake, giving me plenty of time to soak.

With my food in the oven, I light some candles and turn some soothing music on low. If I had a drink and a reading tray to hold my e-reader, I'd be set. Laying my head back on my tub pillow, I shut my eyes and let the world and all my worries melt away as I sink further into the warm bubbles. Until the sound of glass shattering breaks me out of my short-lived tranquility.

I jump out of the tub and wrap my robe around me, not caring that water is dripping all over the floor. I lock the bathroom door and cram myself inside the small towel closet. Well, the bottom half of it. I'm glad I have little stored under the shelves or else I'd never fit in here. Crouched in the dark closet, I keep both my hands twisted on the knob with a death grip, waiting and listening.

"Come out, come out wherever you are," a gruff voice that I don't recognize calls out.

What has Cade got me messed up in? If I make it out of here, I'm going to kill him myself.

Boom. Crack. The bathroom door splinters off the frame, then there's a heavy thud followed by silence.

I hold my breath and count to one hundred while listening for movement. Nothing. Silence follows other than the music I was listening to during my bath. I twist the knob to crack the closet door, but can't get it open very far. It's catching on something. Oh my God. I clamp a palm to my mouth. There's a body. I shove as hard as I can using my feet and get the door cracked enough to shimmy out of it. Blood pools from beneath the side of his face. I'm guessing he must have slipped on the water I got all over the floor. Judging by the way his eyes and mouth are both wide open, he was as shocked as I am.

Pressing two fingers to his neck, I check for a pulse and quickly scurry back, taking in the damage he did to the bathroom door. A sane person would call the police, but I dial the one person I know who will know what to do.

Seth Creed.

CHAPTER TEN

CREED

I've been on the road driving like a bat of hell, breaking every speed limit and traffic law to get to her. I don't know what the fuck happened, but the fear in her voice when she cried my name was all I needed to know. I'll burn the world down to get to her. Whatever it takes, nothing or no one will stand in my way. The second her apartment complex comes into view, I'm parking behind her car and making a mad dash for her door.

By the time I'm there, she's peering out looking for me, having heard my bike.

"Are you okay?" I move inside the doorway, checking her over as I spot the glass shattered on the living room floor. "What happened?"

"There's a dead body in...in my bathroom," she finishes hoarsely.

"Do you know who it is?"

She shakes her head.

"You call the cops or anyone else?"

Another shake.

I pull her into my arms, and she bursts into tears, nuzzling her face deep into my neck as though she can't get close enough. "Hey. I've got you. Always." I kiss the top of her head. "Any idea what this guy wanted?"

"I should have told someone. The other night after I left the clubhouse, I came home and when I climbed into my bed, there was a bullet under my pillow with an X etched on the side. Then tonight Cade showed up outside of the diner when my shift ended."

"Wait. You're telling me that someone left a bullet under your pillow, and you didn't think that was important enough to call the police to report it?"

"Don't be mad." She sniffles.

"I'm not mad at you. Fuck."

"You sound mad."

"Show me the body and tell me what happened."

"He's in here." I follow her to the bathroom in the hall as she continues to explain. "Cade showed up when I was getting off work. He's the guy I told you ghosted me out of the blue. Anyway, he was saying he needed to talk to me, but he was being so weird I just thought he was screwing with me or something. I don't exactly trust a guy who dipped out without a word for weeks. I thought maybe he broke in and left the bullet as a weird joke or something. Before I could get the truth out of him, Chris came out asking if he was bothering me and Cade got spooked and took off. I went by his apartment, but he's moved. Then

I got a text that said sorry. I assumed it was him, since it came from an unknown number. I told him to fuck off and then I came in and started making my dinner and got in the tub for a soak. That's when I heard the glass shatter, and I hid in the towel closet."

"How did he end up dead on the bathroom floor?"

"He slipped on my bathwater. I guess."

"And you have no idea what your ex is mixed up in or why this fucker broke in?"

"Nope."

"Well, we can assume two things. Whoever this guy works for will be waiting to hear from him, and two, when they don't, they'll come looking. Go to your room and pack a bag."

"Shouldn't we call the police?"

"The time to call them has passed since you called me first and it's been hours. Do you trust me?"

"Of course."

"Then let me do this my way." Lottie goes to her room, and I dial Tyrant. "I've got a situation. Clean up. Texting you an address." I tuck my phone back into my pocket and bend down to see who this unlucky bastard is. No wallet. Not even car keys. He's got a tattoo on the inside of his left wrist. A red scorpion. Fucking hell. Some years back, there was a gang that called themselves Hell's Scorpions. When there was a divide in the leadership, they fractured off into The Red Scorpions while the rest remained part of the original group.

Lottie is lucky to be breathing. I didn't think they were even in Alabama and need to tell Havoc about this shit, but first we need to get rid of the body.

Tyrant shows up as fast as he could with two prospects in tow.

"Hey girl," he greets Lottie.

"Hey." She gives him a small wave from where she sits perched on a barstool at the kitchen counter.

"Don't worry. We'll have your place good as new in no time."

She nods but doesn't stop chewing on her thumbnail.

"Keep an eye on her," I tell Henley and Rooster. "Let's step outside a minute." I motion to Tyrant, and he follows me to the end of the breezeway. "Lottie's in danger. I'm taking her to the clubhouse until I can figure out why in the hell she's got a dead Red Scorpion in her bathroom. It's got something to do with her ex. While you and the guys are cleaning up, see if you can find anything that may be hidden in a vent on the wall or something. They've got to think Lottie has something they want."

"I've got you." He bumps his fist against mine.

Lottie doesn't want to leave her car, and I get it. She's independent and needs a safety net. Thinks if she needs to run, she will at least have her wheels. I'll let her make this play, but I'll be taking her keys. I'm pissed that she didn't come to me with this shit in the first place. There's nothing I can do to change it, so we've got to pivot and move forward from where we are now.

I'm following behind her since she's already been to the clubhouse and knows the way. Lying low is what is best given tonight's sequence of events. Seems that's what her ex has been doing. Got himself into some trouble and maybe thought he was protecting Lottie by keeping his distance. Fuck if I know. I'll find out once I track the weasel down. Only a coward would leave his woman unprotected and in the dark.

I get her to my room and she stands with her back pressed to my dresser. The room isn't much, but it's not dirty.

I kick off my boots and hang my cut in the closet before sitting on the edge of the bed. "C'mere, Lottie."

"Is it safe?"

"The fuck does that mean?"

"I don't know who you've fucked in that bed."

"One, you've got no reason to be pulling that jealousy shit right now. Two, my sheets are clean. One of the girls cleaned while I was on the road. Three, I'm not asking."

She scrunches up her nose and starts pacing the length of the room.

"Get your ass over here." I undo my jeans and her eyes go big. "I'm tired, and I'm betting you could use some rest yourself. We can't get answers out of a dead man and if you're right and this has something to do with Cade, chances are he's in hiding. Let's get some rest and I'll have one of my guys trace the number he was texting from. Best-case scenario, we get a location and extract him for questioning. The worst case is Cade goes further underground. Either way, I'll find out who the dead guy was working for and set up a meet to make a deal. But the bottom line is you're safe with me."

She doesn't respond, but I know she's absorbed what I said because she kicks her shoes off and comes to bed. She lays stiffly on the opposite side of the bed, and I roll off the edge to get undressed and flick off the light.

"What are you doing?"

"Told you we're getting some shuteye, beautiful."

"Can't you put on some sweatpants or shorts or something?"

"Nope." I yank my covers back and she curls into herself. "Babe, I'm not going to bite."

"I'm not your babe."

"You sure sounded like you thought you were when you were calling me for help. This kinda favor. You owe me big time and I'll be expecting payment."

"I can hardly wait to hear what you'll be wanting."

"Right now, I want you to relax and not act like you're scared of your own shadow. Promise you. No one will ever lay a hand on you when you're with me or in this clubhouse. You're mine, Lottie, and I think you get what that means."

"I'm not a piece of property."

"In my world you are."

"I live in the real world, Creed. I have rights."

"Never said you didn't, but if you think you'll stand a better chance going this shit alone, I invite you to try to walk out that door and see how far you get before you're calling me again."

"You don't have to be an asshole about it," she snaps.

"If I was being an asshole, I'd have you bent over my knee, spanking your ass for the mess you've gotten yourself entangled in."

"You'd like that, wouldn't you?"

"Damn straight I would because after I was done tanning your hide, I'd fuck that attitude right out of you. You said you needed me, and I drove all damn morning to get to you. Would walk through fire for you."

"Seth," her voice softens.

"Get some sleep, hellcat."

She rolls toward me, placing a hand on my chest. "Thank you."

"You're welcome," I grumble.

I close my eyes, thankful that my blackout curtains are doing their job to keep my room dark.

"I didn't mean to seem ungrateful."

"Go to sleep."

"I can't. Do you think Cade is dead?"

"No. I think that fuckstick got into some shady shit and hung you out to dry."

"What do you mean?"

"We'll talk about it later."

"Tell me now."

"Listen, beautiful. I've had a long fucking night that bled into my morning. It's midday. I've had about two hours of sleep in the past forty-eight hours. If you want to use that mouth, I've got some ideas. Otherwise, I'm about five seconds from passing out and don't even think of trying to leave. I've got your keys, and everyone here knows you're not to go anywhere without my approval."

"Sounds like I'm a prisoner."

"It's how I keep you alive and babe. As much as I like your attitude on a good day, now isn't the time for it."

"Okay."

"Okay," I mutter back, curling an arm around her waist and pulling her back to my front.

"Seth?"

"Shut it."

CHAPTER ELEVEN

Lottie

I awaken, hot and sweaty, pinned to the bed by a bulky body. I rub my eyes, trying to overcome the disoriented sensations I feel as my brain fog caused by sleep dissipates. My throat is dry as the desert. I shift to move out from under Seth's arm and his leg that's slung over mine.

He only curls his arm tighter around my waist and flicks his thumb across my nipple. His erection pokes me in the rear as he murmurs, "quit squirming."

"Um," I whisper. "Can you give me some space?"

"Comfortable," he speaks softly in this sweet sleepy tone I'm not used to him using.

How can I deny him when he's being like this? It's been years, and he still knows how to charm my panties off. I'm not mad about it, though. I could have worse prospects. I'm mentally drained after the night or day I had. I don't even know what time it is. "Shit," I hiss, shoving him back. "I need to get ready for work."

"You're not going to work."

"I can't just not show up."

"That's exactly what you're going to do. Whoever is after you is going to know by now that their guy failed. Where do you think they are going to look for you first or second?"

"I need to warn Tonya."

"Ghoul will worry about Tonya."

"If trouble lands on her door because of me..."

"She's in a safe place. Her and her kid."

"How do you know that?"

"Because I got up to take a leak and filled him in. You don't have to worry, but if you're going to call in, use my burner." He reaches over the edge of the bed and grabs a cellphone from one of the pockets of his jeans.

I put in a call to work and leave a message for Carl saying that I'm sick and need to take my sick days. It's the best I can do right now. Seeth takes possession of his cell phone back and hooks his arm back around me, pressing his lips to the back of my neck. His hand resumes the position of cupping my breast.

"I'm not having sex with you," I warn.

"We'll see about that." I can feel his lips curving into a smile against my skin as he slides his hand down my belly and inside my sweatpants.

"Stop it." I grab his hand and try to prevent him from going any lower.

"Give me one good reason."

"I don't know. Because someone out there wants to kill me."

"We don't know that they want you dead."

"Geez, that's so reassuring. Thank you. Now excuse me while I take my panties off."

"Okay."

"Ugh." I move to slide out from under his hold, but he won't let me go. "You're annoying."

"Sometime but currently, I want to fuck you."

"Oh my God."

"No, but if that's what you want to call me, I'm not going to correct you."

"I hate you."

He shoves his hand into my underwear and touches me between my legs. "Survey says that's a lie."

"Would you stop?"

"Nope." He rolls over top of me, gazing down at me all cocky. "My soul has been burning for yours for ten years, hellcat. I'm not letting you get away a third time." He angles his head as his lips descend on mine, and I'm powerless to stop him. I don't want to. He starts out soft and slow, kissing me, closed mouthed. I surrender to him, to the passion his touch fuels inside me.

I'd be a liar if I said I haven't dreamed of this. Of him a million times, wondering if it'd be just as good. It's even better. I'm more experienced and so is he. Creed takes his time, kissing me deep with lots of tongue. His hands are on me, yanking at my clothes and at the moment I'm very appreciative of the fact that he slept with only his boxer briefs, allowing me access to all of him with nothing to get in my way of exploring his muscular form. I don't think there's ever been a more beautiful man than Seth Creed.

Our bodies meld and move together as we taste and rediscover one another. Everything going on, all the noise in the back of mind, it all fades to black. All that exists is this moment between us. As though time itself has stopped.

Memories of what we once were are being replaced by what we are now and thoughts of what we can be if given the chance, and I want it. I want it all. I want him and the life that was promised. This cocky biker that kisses me like nobody's business.

That touches my body in all the right spots.

This man that was made to love me and only me.

I know it deep in my heart of hearts that he's mine and deep down I've always been his.

We fit like two pieces of one whole being.

"You gonna let me get a taste?" He moves down my body, lifting my hips to slip my underwear down my legs.

Oh yeah. He can have any part of me he wants as long as he keeps his mouth and hands on me.

There's never been anything or anyone better than this. Better than him.

Pushing my knees apart, he goes right for what he wants. He's all fingers and tongue, working my pussy overtime. No one knows or can do me better.

"Fuck me, hellcat. Better than I remember." He delves his tongue inside me while circling my clit with his fingers. I pinch my nipples as my hips and back arch up off the mattress, doing my best not to cry out.

Creed shoves his fingers in my mouth, giving me a taste of how wet and turned on I am for him. The act is intimate and erotic, making me want his cock in my mouth instead. I moan around his fingers like I would if I were sucking him off.

"Need inside you, Lottie." He reaches over into the nightstand for a condom. I watch excitedly as he rips the foil wrapper open with his teeth. As soon as he gets it on, he's lining up with my slick entrance and with one harsh thrust, he's rooted inside me to the damn hilt. His darkened green eyes meet mine and then the moment is ruined by a knock at his door.

"Yo, Creed. You in there?"

"Don't you dare stop."

"Come back in ten minutes," he groans.

"You can fuck her later. We've got church."

"Fuck." He presses his lips to my throat.

"Church? Now hardly seems like the time to pray."

He chuckles. "Means Prez has called a meeting. And it's disrespectful to make him wait."

"And what about me? You're just going to leave me here to finish myself off?"

"When Prez kills me, just remember I gave you a great orgasm," he tells me before claiming my lips to finish what he started.

"Let me on top and I promise your punishment will be well worth your reward," I promise. He rolls us over and I straddle his hips, bouncing my ass against his thighs as I grind down on his cock, wanting nothing more than to get him off. "Are you clean?"

"Yeah, why?"

"Good." I ease off him and remove the condom. "Because we'll both come a lot faster now."

"You're going to be the death of me."

"Not today, at least." I circle my hips, spelling out our names. "Not yet."

"I'm about to come, baby." He slaps my ass and gives my left cheek a good squeeze. I wrap my hand around his throat, nearly choking the life out of him as we both get off.

His warmth sticks to my inner thighs as I ride the last waves of pleasure. My body does a shudder and I fall forward, pressing my chest to his with him still inside me.

"Fuck." He hugs me tight and presses his lips to my shoulder. "I've gotta go. I won't be long."

"I'll be around. Maybe." I smirk, sated as a cat who got to lick the cream.

Creed left me alone to go to his meeting or whatever. I'm not brave enough to leave the privacy his room affords me. I don't know anyone here or how receptive they will be with the trouble I've likely brought to their door.

I shiver at the memory of seeing that guy dead on my bathroom floor. It was a freak accident. Even if he was trespassing, I don't think the dude deserved to die, unless he was there to hurt me or, worse, take my life. Then, in that case, I'd call what he got karma. Why was he there in the first place and what does all of this have to do with Cade? The more I think about the whole situation, the more pissed off I get.

I dig around in the bag I packed until I find my cell phone. My battery needs to charge. I nose around Creed's room, looking for a charging cord and block. The drawer of his nightstand practically explodes with condoms when I open it. The sight shouldn't irritate me, but it does. How many women has he brought back to this room to fuck? Is he having that much sex that he warrants having a hundred rubbers next to his bed? Suddenly, our heated moment of passion seems weak and cheap. I am afraid of what else I will find if I poke around in his dresser. For all I know, he's got a whole stash of sex toys or something.

I can't sit here and do nothing. I use his bathroom to wash up and change my clothes. I half expect the door to be locked from the outside when I go to exit his room, but it's open and no one is guarding it to keep me from leaving.

I find my way to the bar area where a guy with a blue mohawk is behind the bar. I faintly remember seeing him at my apartment. I don't know if it would be weird to thank him for helping dispose of the body in my apartment and cleaning up the evidence. I'm sure there's a don't ask, don't tell code that applies to the situation. I don't want him to think I'm unappreciative. I know he took a risk, and he doesn't know me.

"You look like you could use a coffee." Another prospect by the name of Asphalt with gorgeous olive skin and green eyes that could rival Creed's hands me a mug. "This will cure anything. Trust me."

I take a cautious sip, surprised at how good it tastes. "Mmm. That's delicious. Thank you."

"Anytime."

"So, this is the one Creed's been pinning after," one of the women I noticed here the other night says.

"Excuse me?"

The dude with the Mohawk coughs and makes a cut it out motion with his hand slicing across his throat.

"I thought you were married with a baby." She tucks her pink hair behind her ear and leans across the bar to steal some strawberries.

"Ignore Kitty. She doesn't know what she's talking about," Asphalt says with a smile, but I can tell he doesn't quite believe his own words.

"You thought I was who?" I press.

She shrugs, having read the room. "Nothing."

"Right. Can one of you tell Creed I need my keys and I need to borrow this?" I go straight for the phone charger behind the bar. I don't wait for any of them to argue. I take my coffee with me back to his room because I'm not wasting good coffee.

I plug in my phone and gather my belongings. I will text Cade and sort this out, and Creed can be hung up on some married chick all he wants. I don't do second place. Not anymore. He did that to me one too many times when we were secretly hooking up. I'm not that timid girl who will lap up whatever attention he deems fit to give me. I won't compete for his affection.

Fuck that.

If he wants further payment for helping me out, then he can bill me.

I grab my phone and see if it has enough juice to turn on. While I wait for my screen to boot up, I snoop even though I know I shouldn't.

There's a laptop on top of the dresser and I hope it has charge.

I take it to the bed with me and sip on my coffee. Before I go, I'll have to ask Asphalt what he does to make his brew this tasty. The computer wants a pin number. I try his birth date and its invalid. I don't think it would be his father's, but I give it a test anyway. Nope. Hmm. I'm desperate and delusional but enter my own and voila. I sit stunned that it actually unlocked the screen.

I don't understand men at all.

AT ALL.

I open the browser to check my social media and his account pops right up and logged in. A good person would log out or go to an incognito window, except I'm a glutton for punishment and wonder how many women he talks to. I know whatever I find will result in me hurting my own feelings. Yet I can't look away. He's not messaged with anyone in months, and he only has one new notification, which means maybe he doesn't use the profile often. I'm aware this is a such a breach in trust and invasion of privacy and if I asked, he'd probably tell me to go for it. He's never lied to me about other women. That doesn't make the sting burn any less.

I click on his profile. He doesn't post much. A few pictures of his motorcycle. Selling bike parts. Normal biker guy stuff. But it's the person who likes all his posts that catches my attention. Her name is Ember, and she resembles me too closely for comfort. Dark hair. Blue eyes. She's gorgeous. I click her profile and my heart stops. He commented on her last photo. 'Happy looks good on you, beautiful.' He called her beautiful like he does me. It shouldn't cut me this deep, but the blade is piercing my heart. Tears form and I bite my bottom lip hard enough to draw blood.

She's holding a baby and wears a wedding ring.

"So this is the one Creed's been pinning after?"

"I thought you were married with a baby."

I click see all comments to see if she replied to him. She only hearted it.

I don't know what to think. I mean, I expected that there might be someone and know he's no choir boy. But a married woman with a child? Is the baby his? Does he love her?

I swipe a stray tear from my cheek when Creed barges into his room. "Heard you were asking for your keys." He stops at the end of the bed. "Why are you crying?"

"It's nothing. I just want to go home."

"Beautiful, you know that's not going to happen."

I slam his computer shut. "Don't call me that," I snap.

"Okay. I've clearly missed something, so why don't you dial your tone back and tell me what the fuck has you ready to rip my throat out?"

"Fuck you. Give me my keys."

"Not happening. I prefer you here in my bed, all in one piece, all sexy, even if you're pissed off at me for whatever reason."

"Don't. You can't charm your way out of this."

"All right. Talk to me." He sits at the foot of the bed, pulling my feet into his lap. I scooch back against the headboard, away from his touch. "What the fuck, Lottie? An hour ago, you were begging me to fuck you and now I can't touch you?"

He goes for his computer, and I jump up off the bed. He changes targets and gets hold of me, tugging me back down on the bed.

I elbow him in the ribs and debate head-butting him with the back of my head, but I don't want to hurt him. I only want him to let me go.

"You can try to run from me, Lottie, but I'll always catch you. I'll always find you. I love you and nothing you do or say is going to change that or stop me from proving it. No matter what it takes. So you can fight me. Bite me. Punch me. I don't care. I'm going to keep coming at you until you submit, because we both know that despite whatever this tantrum is, you love me, too."

Chapter Twelve

CREED

Lottie stops fighting against me, either because she's giving in or she's grown tired. Either way, she's still in my arms and if that makes me a dick, I don't give a fuck.

"Is this about what Kitty said?"

"Yes, and no. It's everything, Creed. You have a bazillion condoms in your nightstand. You're apparently obsessed with a woman that's married with a child who looks oddly similar to me but prettier. Is that your kid? I don't know anything about you. I mean, you belong to an outlaw club who has the means to show up and dispose of a body in broad daylight. Like, who even are you?"

"Seems we need to set some shit straight." I loosen my hold on her, but she doesn't pull away. I take it as a good sign to keep talking. "The condoms are there if I need them. I practice safe sex. I like to fuck. I'm not ashamed of it. The other guys around here love pussy, too. It's not a bad thing to have plenty of protection for anyone who needs it. The guys know they can always count on me having a stash in my room, so if they need it, they can come grab whatever they need."

"Okay. That's smart."

"Damn right it is. You wouldn't believe the bitches trying to pin a kid on a brother because they'll do anything to be an ol' lady. And yeah, Ember is gorgeous. We had a fling, and that's all it was. I'm friend with her and her man. The kid is his. I check in sometimes on how they are doing and give him shit about if he's not treating her right that I'll step in, but beautiful." She freezes up and I look at my laptop lying on the opposite side of the bed. "You don't like me calling you that because you saw I said it to Ember. It's just a term of endearment, same as calling someone honey or babe."

Lottie scowls up at me and wiggles out of my arms.

"Okay. I get that means something to you, but you're the only woman I call hellcat. But if that other shit bothers you, I'll make a conscious effort to stop doing it. If it means something to you, then it's important to me that I respect that boundary." Her expression softens, so I keep going. "You know who I am." I press her palm to my chest over my heart. "You know me the same as I know you. But you're right that there are things you don't know about me and if this is going to work, you've got to know those parts too and learn to accept them. I used to have trouble controlling my temper and, as you know, I'd fight to get that aggression out. I take jobs that involve me doing stuff that I know you

116

might hate me for, but I'm good at it. I make damn good money. Enough that if you're with me, you won't have to lift a finger if you don't want to, but being with me comes with a lot of responsibilities and you being okay with there being some shit I can't share."

"I need a minute," she tells me, and I give her that space even though we really don't have the time for it. There are things we found out about Cade that she needs to be aware of. Her pretty blue eyes meet mine. "I understand a lot of what you're saying. It's a lot to take stock of."

"Yeah. I'm sure you've got more questions and I'll answer them, but there is something else we need to discuss."

"Okay." She sits up straighter, appearing calmer.

"This Cade pussy. What did he tell you his job was?"

"A delivery driver for fast food and sometimes he'd do taxi type stuff."

"He ever tell you he was dealing drugs for the Red Scorpions?"

"Say what?"

"He's a drug mule, and he stole from them. Hid a flash drive in the heater vent of your bathroom wall that had evidence against the gang because they murdered his friend because he let him take the fall. He used you like he did his buddy and put your life in danger. I'll tell you what the pissed off side of me wants to do. If it was up to me, I'd hand him and the drive over. Let them figure their own shit out as long as they never breathe your direction again.

Option two, the flash drive gets destroyed and I give my assurance to Red that he's got nothing to worry about and if they catch Cade, that's on him. Option three, I go to war with these fuckers and take them all out. Cade included."

"Won't they be mad about the dead guy?"

"It's a price we all pay in the underground world. They know it. I know it. You've gotta learn to live with it. Can't save everyone, baby. But I can damn sure do whatever it takes to make sure you're covered."

"If you give Cade to them, they will kill him."

"Normally I'd give a fuck, but he lost that chance the minute he hid that shit in your apartment and made you their target."

"We don't know they were going to kill me."

"They left a hitman calling card under your pillow. I know what that shit means because it's what I do, Lottie. I kill pieces of shit for a living."

"You what?" All color drains from her face as she stares at me.

"You heard what I said. You don't have to agree with what I do, but I need you to understand the men I kill aren't good people."

"I. I don't even know what to say right now. I feel sick."

I move in to comfort her, and she flinches. "I can't touch you now? Are you scared of me?"

"I don't know, Creed. You just told me you murder people for money. You play God." She shifts her shoulders and makes a face like I disgust her. Maybe I do, but I can't change who I am.

"I think I like it better when you call me Seth."

Tears pool in her eyes.

"Hey, look at me." I twist her face toward me. "I'm still the same man. The one you grew up with. The one you first gave yourself to. The one you've always loved."

Lottie licks her lips.

"Tell me you understand. That you accept me as I am."

Her mouth opens but no words come out and I'm afraid I've lost her when I barely just got her back. But then her lips find mine, frantic and hungry.

"There will never be a version of you I don't want. That I won't accept. Only thing I can't take is losing you again. I'm all in with you. No matter the price."

"Good." I hold her down on the bed, claiming her.

Body.

Heart.

Mind.

And soul.

All that she is, is mine for the taking.

"Let's get one more thing straight." I hold her gaze. "No one could ever compare to the beauty that is you. I loved you first and I'm going to love you last. Anything that came between then and now doesn't matter. Inconsequential."

"Ditto," she whispers into my mouth as she delves her tongue between the seam of my lips. "No more talking, honey." She squeezes my ass over my jeans.

"Most beautiful woman I've ever laid eyes on."

"For someone who loves to give orders, you don't receive them very well."

"Nope." I grin and remove her shirt. I yank a lacey cup of her bra down, exposing her nipple so I can swirl my tongue around it till the skin turns taught. "I like this." I tug the other cup down, repeating motion with the other, getting my first proper look at her skeletal sternum tattoo, that spans beneath her breasts. "Did it hurt?"

"Nothing I couldn't handle."

"Fucking sexy, hellcat."

"You know I don't remember you being this chatty back in the day."

"That's because I was focused on one thing."

"And what was that?"

"Coming." She yanks my hair, and I laugh against her stomach as I tongue her navel ring. I didn't even notice it earlier. I was so determined to be inside her. This time around, I'm going slow. Memorizing and tasting every inch of her skin. Reclaiming what's mine and only mine.

"Don't worry, I'll be sure to get you off multiple times to make up for it."

"You've incurred a debt much higher than a couple of orgasms."

"That so?" I press my lips to her stomach. "Maybe it's the other way around and you're indebted to me for all the blow jobs you teased me with and never delivered on."

"Ha. You're funny."

"Sometimes." I trail my tongue further down as I undo the button on her jeans and unzip them. I work the denim down her legs and fling them against the wall, not caring where they land. I start to go down on my woman when she stops me, tipping a finger under my chin and lifting my gaze. "It's you who needs to submit. Time to repay that debt I owe." She licks her lips.

My hellcat wants to suck my cock.

Lottie takes charge, and I lay back and let her treat my body like her wonderland as she grips the bottom of my shaft with her fist and wraps that sweet mouth around the head. She knows how to use that tongue. Gliding it up and down the underside back around to the front licking me like her personal lollipop, stretching her lips wide to accommodate my size. The inside of her mouth is like warm velvet. Her movements are calculated and sensual, but I want my hellcat to get hers, too.

"Get up here and sit on my face."

No hesitation, like a good girl. She does as she's told, smothering me in her pussy. The way Lottie smells when she's turned on is addictive. She's addictive and I'll never be able to get enough of her sweetness. I grip her hips, holding her where I want her, tongue fucking her hole until she's coming on my face as she takes my dick to the back of her throat. Her body trembles and shakes as she gags on me, but I don't let up and neither does she.

Chapter Thirteen

Lottie

"Oh God. Oh God." I pant as Creed slams into me from behind.

"That's right, beautiful. I'm your God and tonight you'll pay worship to this cock that owns you."

I grip the edge of the mattress so close to finding my bliss, but every time I am about to come, he pulls out and spanks my ass and my pussy. Showing me no mercy with every savage slap and thrust, as he fucks me like an unhinged animal. Sweat drips down my back and to the crack of my ass as he pulls out, only to slam back in.

Curving an arm around my waist, he pulls me upright to where I'm sitting on his thighs, back pressed to his chest. Our bodies stick together as I grind on his lap, feeling his dick twitching and pulsing inside me.

"You feel that, Lottie. Your pussy is choking the life outta my cock. Come for me. Come all over this cock." His lips meet the sweet spot between my neck and shoulder as he pinches one of my nipples with one hand and rubs my clit with the other. "You're taking me so good. So good. Fucking tightest pussy. So wet. I'm gonna come. Keep fucking me like that right there." My dirty talking biker bites my neck, marking me with the imprint of his teeth. I know it will leave a bruise, but I don't care. I want everyone to know I'm his and he's mine. His body does a jolt, and his warmth coats my inner walls.

Even though he's just gotten off, he maneuvers me where he wants me, putting me in the missionary position to make sure I get mine. Arms hooked under my knees, he lifts my ass and angles me so that every stroke of his cock hits the right spot every time.

I'm unraveling and unable to focus on anything but the burning in my lower belly as stars explode behind my eyes.

He pulls out and pushes two fingers inside me, forcing me to orgasm again and again till I'm squirting. My juices gush over his fingers as they continue to curl inside me. And when I think I can't take anymore, he shoves those same fingers in my mouth and proceeds to eat me out again until I'm a blubbering mess, crying out, consumed by pure ecstasy.

One second, I'm still coming and the next thing I know is he's got me in the shower, bathing me.

"There she is. Thought I fucked you into a coma." He grins, appearing quite proud of the fact that's exactly what he did. "Didn't want to wake you, but there's something we've gotta do. Cade's here. Ghoul tracked his ass down."

"What are you going to do with him?"

"Make him watch me fuck you so he can be reminded firsthand of what he gave up and fumbled on."

"Yeah no. That's not happening."

He mutters something under his breath beneath the spray of the water that I can't understand. "While you were sleeping, I cut a deal. Not one I preferably am happy with, but it's one I can live with."

"What are you going to do with him?"

"You'll see."

I'm not sure I like the sound of that. Sure, I don't want Cade back and he's a dick, but I don't wish him harm or worse. Death.

Once we're both dressed, Creed escorts me out behind the clubhouse to a wooded area. We enter a clearing between some trees where some of the other club members have Cade on his knees at gunpoint.

There's a man dressed in an expensive suit who would be handsome if it wasn't for the scar running diagonally down the left side of his face partially through both his eye and his lips like someone tried to slice his face in half. With him are two guys dressed in all black, similar to the one who broke into my apartment.

"I'm sorry, Lottie. I never meant to involve you."

"Shut the fuck up," Rogue grits out, before smacking Cade in the back of the head in warning. "No one told you to speak."

"I hear you have something that belongs to me," the man in the suit states, then nods toward Creed.

"I have the drive. Cade has given his word for whatever its worth that there aren't any copies. In exchange for his freedom, you'll get the drive and his laptop. And for facilitating this deal, the club gets fifteen percent of your sales for the next twelve months. You'll also forgo any retaliation for the death of your man, since it was his own stupidity that got him killed. You ever so much as breathe near my woman again, I'll kill you myself."

I don't know if his threat is meant for the man in the suit or for Cade. Maybe both. Creed shakes the drug dealer's hand and gives him the drive. All I know is I'm glad this is over.

"What's going to happen to Cade?"

"Don't fucking care, but I won't be surprised if he's found in a landfill or simply disappears all together for good."

"And you think that guy will keep his word?"

He lifts a shoulder. "Can't say. That's a future problem. He won't want any trouble. If he's smart, he's realized we gave him a copy of Cade's drive and if he fucks us, we'll use the original however we need to."

"I see."

"I give you my word that whatever fate awaits Cade, it won't be at my hands."

"Thank you."

"Anything for you, hellcat."

"I'll take my keys now."

"Real cute that you think you're going anywhere."

"I've got a job to get back to and a life."

"I told you. There's no reason for you to work unless you really want to."

"It's a sweet offer, but I can't sit around all day waiting for you to call between jobs."

"I want to start a life together."

"I'm not saying no."

"Not sounding like a yes."

"Relationships are about compromising."

"I can be persuasive."

"Oh yeah."

"Yeah." He comes in close, dipping his head down to kiss me. "Come on. There's something I want to show you." He leads me to a distinct part of the property where there's different plots of land reserved for what appears to be cabins. "Tyrant and Blair have their place over there. And this is going to be ours."

"Ours?" my stomach does a pitch.

"Not losing any more time with you."

"You're moving way too fast. I'm not ready."

"So what? We waste our time with me sleeping at your place when I'm in town during the week and on weekends you'll sleep at the clubhouse with me until the build is complete? Lugging shit back and forth or buying double when it could be solved by you staying here with me."

"It's not that simple."

"It is if you want it to be. Cabin will be ready to live in within two months, tops."

"Okay. So, what's wrong with us dating until then? I like my apartment."

"It's not safe."

"It was until a few days ago. Now the threat is over."

"I claimed you as mine to the leader of the Red Scorpions. You think that doesn't put an even bigger target on your back if he retaliates against me or the club?"

"Well, geez. When you put it like that Creed, I can't wait to move in with you."

"Don't be like that. You should be aware, is all."

"And if I don't want any of it?"

"You don't want to be with me?"

"Of course I do, you idiot."

"Jesus fuckin' Christ, Lottie. You're giving me a fucking headache."

"If you'll give me my keys, I'll cure it for you real quick."

"Pain in my ass, you know that."

"You're an asshole."

"Get used to it because this asshole is yours."

I smirk and burst out laughing. "Is that so?"

"Not like that. Ain't nobody touching my ass. Not even you."

"What if it's like a little surprise one day and you like it?"

"You shove your finger in my ass and I'm going to put my dick in yours."

"You never know, you might like it. A lot of guys do."

He stomps off back toward the clubhouse.

"What's your problem?" I practically have to run to keep up with him.

He stops so abruptly that I practically run into his back as he turns to face me, all red-faced like a raging bull. "You think I want to hear how you've stuck your finger in some other guy's asshole, and he liked it?"

I can't stop laughing. He looks ridiculous. Even the tips of his ears are red. Like steam is going to blow out at any second.

"Do you see me laughing? It's not funny, Lottie."

"Are you jealous? You're insane. I think you might be certifiable. And for your information, I was teasing you."

"You being with other men isn't something I find entertaining."

"Okay, big guy. Noted."

"Don't call me big guy."

"Whatever. Have your man period or whatever this whole mood swing you've got going is. I'm going home."

"You want your keys?" he yells at me.

"I do."

"Too fucking bad."

"You're being childish."

"Come on. Let's get your shit. I'll follow you to make sure you get there safe and sound."

"Don't do me any favors."

"Think we're already past that. I got your little boyfriend out of trouble for you. Is that what this is? You want to get back with him?"

"What? Where do you even come up with this shit? Are you hearing yourself? I hurt your feelings. I'm sorry. I just need time to process everything. You scare me, Seth."

"Either you want this, or you don't. There's no having one foot in the door and the other ready to run at the first sign of trouble."

"You should talk about running and pushing people away. That's you. Not me."

"I apologized."

"Good."

"Fine."

"Fine."

"Fuck me. Always got to have the last word, don't you?"

"No."

He throws his hands up.

"Are you done? I'm getting hungry and you owe me a dinner date."

Suddenly he charges at me, dipping down, shoving a shoulder into my waist as he takes me over that shoulder, hanging me upside down, my head reaching his lower back.

"Put me down."

"Quiet, Lottie."

Chapter Fourteen

CREED

I enter the clubhouse with Lottie banging her fists on my back like a spoiled ass child and everyone is sitting around the tv drinking, but all their eyes are fixed on us. "What?" I grumble and Country chuckles.

"Enjoying the show you two are putting on."

"Don't you fuckers have some toilets to scrub or something?"

Rooster whistles and resumes his position behind the bar.

I take Lottie to the kitchen and sit her on the counter. She doesn't argue. She sits quietly while I grab the cheese and butter from the fridge. Going through the motions of lightly greasing the pan and turning the stove on, I butter the bread and add garlic salt to the spread. Lottie's favorite comfort food has always been a garlic grilled cheese with provolone and colby jack.

"You remembered." Her tone comes out softer and sweeter.

"I remember how to handle you when you get hangry. I remember everything about you."

"How to handle me?" She purses her lips, and I can tell it's to prevent herself from smarting off.

"Yeah, babe. Going to feed you, then fuck the rest of that attitude out of you."

"Ha. Who said anything about letting you back in my panties?"

"You can pretend all you want to that you're going to deny me, but I bet when I drive you home, my motorcycle won't be the only thing that's purring. My baby has claws. A true hellcat."

"You're so full of it. You don't know when to quit, do you?"

"Go ahead, deny it."

"Shut up and make my sandwich, and you better have ketchup."

"Bossy," I mutter but crack a smile and glance at her out the corner of my eye as she hops off the counter and goes to the fridge to help herself to a can of Coke.

Minutes later, she's sheathed her claws and is disgustingly dipping her sandwich in ketchup.

"I don't remember inviting you to stay." Lottie bats her lashes at me from her preferred side of her bed.

After feeding her, I returned her keys and followed her back to her place. This isn't going to work if I steam roll her at every turn. She's always had a streak of independence about her.

"I don't recall asking permission."

"And you call me bossy."

I grunt as I look for somewhere to lay my cut and settle for folding it over the footboard of the bed.

"You can hang it in the closet if you'd rather it not get knocked to the floor."

I don't comment on how she wants to give me space in her closet, but doesn't want me spending the night. "Do you have a spare toothbrush, or should I use yours?"

"Second drawer of the bathroom vanity and absolutely do not use my toothbrush." She makes a gagging expression of sticking her finger in her mouth.

"Can stick my tongue in your ass, but don't touch your toothbrush. Got it."

"Maybe don't talk either."

In the bathroom, I glance up from pissing to see Lottie standing in the doorway watching me.

"You want to hold it for me, make sure I don't piss on the seat?"

"Funny. I need to brush my teeth too. And you could have closed the door."

"I wasn't expecting a viewing party."

"I'm going to smother you with my pillow."

"I'd go happily if it were your pussy instead."

"You're literally the worst."

I give my dick a shake and flush. After washing my hands, we stand at the sink, brushing our teeth, her elbow digging into my side, but staring at our reflection I feel content for the first time in a long motherfucking time.

The guys did an excellent job cleaning up. You'd never know that there had been a dead body on the floor nor a pool of blood. They even replaced her sliding glass door in the living room and, of course, the one in the bathroom.

In her bed, I pull her into my hold, our bodies curving together perfectly.

"If I haven't told you," Lottie whispers, "thank you."

"For what?"

"Everything. Loving me when I'm not very lovable."

"You don't need to thank me, beautiful. I'm exactly where I want to be. Well, almost." I slide my palm into her panties, cupping her between the legs.

"Isn't this fucking sweet?" an unfamiliar voice pierces the room as the sound of a gun being cocked fills my ears. "Don't bother getting up."

"Cade? What are you doing here?"

"Did he just come out of the closet?"

"I'll ask the questions. I'm the one with the gun."

"I thought you had the locks changed."

"No. I had a text. They can't get anyone over here until next week sometime."

"Hello." Cade waves his pistol around.

"Is that a toy?"

"I don't know," Lottie tells me.

"What the fuck is wrong with you two?"

"Look, man. I saved your life."

"Fuck you. You both ruined everything. I had him. He was going to pay for what he did."

"So what? You're going to hurt Lottie, whose only fault was ever trusting you?"

"No. You're going to give me the copy of the drive. I know you made one. Guys like you aren't stupid."

"Is that all you want? It's in my pants pocket." I hold my hands up, pretending I'm not a threat.

"Cade, maybe you should go."

"No one asked you." He points his weapon at Lottie and that's when I begin to lose my cool.

"Don't point that thing unless you intend to use it. First rule of owning a gun."

"I should shoot you both."

"If you're going to do it, may I suggest you take me out first because if you shoot Lottie first..."

"Hey." She punches me in the shoulder.

"You guys aren't listening. What the fuck is wrong with you?" he turns the gun on me, which is where I'd rather he point it if he's going to aim it as someone.

"A lot, but I was just saying if you shoot her first, that gives me time to take you out before you go for me."

"I mean, you should take his advice. Creed offs people for a living."

"He does what?"

"It's true."

"I'm going to shoot myself if the two of you don't shut up." He aims the gun at his temple and brings his hand down and the gun fires, blowing his right upper ear off.

"Did he just..." Lottie stares at me with her mouth open as Cade touches the side of his head, then looks at the blood on his fingers that's also sprayed all over the wall behind him.

"I think he's going to pass out," she says as I ease off the bed and take the gun from him.

"Get a towel, beautiful. And maybe a bowl of ice."

She nods and runs out of the room.

"How bad is it?" Cade asks.

"Could be worse. You almost blew your own brains out."

"Am I going to die?"

138

"I'm no doctor."

"Didn't she say you do this stuff professionally?"

"Yeah, but when I shoot, it's to kill. You'd do well to remember that in case you walk out of here and think about getting more ideas, yeah?"

"I've got a towel, and I called 911." Lottie hands the towel to Cade and he presses it to the side of his head where his ear should be.

"Hey. I don't feel so good." He falls back into the wall, and we help him slide down to the floor.

"What should I do with the ice?" Lottie asks.

"Do you know if they can reattach an ear?"

"What?"

I nod to the partial bit of what's left on the floor.

"Oh." Lottie's face screws into a pinched expression and then she's running to the bathroom to throw up.

The EMT's show up a few minutes later and load Cade up in the ambulance to take him to the hospital. I may have also told them he was trying to kill himself in front of us because Lottie dumped him to get with me and how he left a bullet under her pillow as a threat. So if he tries saying shit about me, they will think he's just nuts and having a mental health break. Other than his injury, the dude should recover. Having a fucked up ear is enough punishment for his stupidity, but he tries to pull anything again or even looks at Lottie. I won't hesitate to kill him.

"You okay?" I hug Lottie to my chest as the ambulance pulls away, followed by the police officer who came to investigate. I gave him Cade's gun. If they have any sense, they won't let him have it back.

She's still shaken from the whole situation, but holds back from crying. "So I was thinking..."

"You want to stay at the clubhouse with me?"

"Mhmm. You know I don't really like my apartment that much, anyway."

"The bedroom could really use a paint job," I tell her and she lets out a giggle.

"Oh my god. That's so mean."

"It's true."

I take my woman home with me and get her settled for the night.

"You should probably call and cancel the lock change and just terminate your lease."

"I will."

"Did you just agree with me?"

"Don't gloat," she warns.

"Hmm." I nuzzle her neck and kiss the base of her throat, tickling her skin with my tongue.

"Love you, Seth." Her words warm my soul and everything in my world feels right as rain on a hot summer night.

"Back at you."

"Ugh. Don't say it like that."

"So now you want to argue about how I say I love you."

My chest rumbles as I erupt with laughter.

"I hate you."

"Is that so?"

"Yeah," she sneers, trying to roll away from me.

"Well, baby. I love the hell outta you. Let me show you how much." I roll over her on my bed, looming over her. I go in for a kiss and she bites me on the lip. "Fuck, you're cute when you're pissed."

"No, I'm not."

"Yeah, you are. Look." I angle her head and force her to take in our reflection in the mirror on the back of my closet door. Her eyes soften and she melts beneath me. I hold her gaze there in the mirror. "I love you, Charlotte Rae Pierce." A tear rolls down her cheek. "Don't cry, baby."

"I never thought I'd have this again." She laces our fingers together. "I only ever want to do life with you. No matter how messed up or crazy it gets, as long as I have this. You. Every night."

"You've got me. Always." I press my lips to hers and I spend the rest of the night making soft and sweet love to my woman.

Epilogue

Lottie

Sometime later

My heart thumps wildly in my chest as I exit the diner to see Creed parked across the street on his Harley looking every bit the devil I know him to be.

His dark shades mask his eyes, but I know he's staring at me full of love. His leather jacket is unzipped to reveal a black tee that clings to the sculpted muscles of his chest. The rugged beard that frames his lips is new, giving him a dangerous appeal that sends a shiver down my spine.

"Hey handsome," I comment, keeping my voice steady as I approach him, hoping I'm hiding how nervous I am.

He grins at me, a flash of white teeth against his tan skin. "You ready?"

I look back at the diner, having worked my last shift seeing Tonya watch us leave while probably trying not to cry. She's a hormonal mess, but she's also five months pregnant with Ghoul's baby. I guess some people really can change. Since he found out that he's going to be a father, he's really stepped up for her and for Kaydence. I'm glad she has him. He's not as bad as I thought.

"I can't believe I'm doing this," I mutter under my breath before turning back to Creed to accept the helmet he's holding out for me.

"That makes two of us."

"Are you having second thoughts?"

"Nope. You?"

"No."

"Good." He presses his lips to mine, then makes sure my helmet is tight enough, but not too tight, before we ride off into the sunset.

Well, heading for Las Vegas to the same chapel Tyrant and Blair were married in. Things seemed to work out for them, so we thought, why not? At least if we don't kill each other before we get there.

The wind whips my hair around and tugs at my clothes. The only sounds are the rumble of the engine beneath us and my heartbeat thudding wildly inside my chest.

We're really doing it.

Getting our happily ever after.

Creed's giving me the beautiful life he promised me years ago when I was still a girl, and he was barely a man. I pledged myself to him one stormy night in my bedroom, not understanding it would one day lead us here, but I had hoped, dreamed, and even prayed for it.

I can't predict what the future holds for us, but whatever is waiting for us, I know we'll tackle it head on together. I scratch my nails against his stomach and smile.

I'm going to marry this man.

This scary over the top alpha who kills evil men for a living.

I'm going to be his wife.

His forever.

DEAR READER,

I hope you enjoyed Creed and Lottie's story.

Creed was first introduced in my Royal Bastards MC: Charleston, WV series in Taming The Biker and he appeared in The Biker's Vow. I fell in love with him and knew he needed his own book. I rewrote the start of this book so many times I lost count and cut some scenes that I hated to lose but they didn't fit. I may post them on my website or through my newsletter when I get more time to clean them up. Their ride went way different than I planned and between having emergency surgery and life's other curveballs I wasn't going to argue with Creed. He'd win anyway.

If you want more Kings of Carnage be sure to check out the rest of the authors from the Alabama chapter.

Alabama officers: Hilary Storm (Havoc), Sapphire Knight (Tyrant), Glenna Maynard (Creed),Chelsea Camaron (Rogue)

Much love and happy reading!

Glenna

About Glenna

Glenna Maynard is a Wall Street Journal & USA Today Bestselling Author best known for her gritty motorcycle club romances. She has a passion for writing antiheroes and romance as dark as her heart with over 60 titles published. When she isn't arguing with the voices in her head or drinking reader tears you can find her curled up with a good book or attempting a new craft with her kids and husband in Eastern Kentucky.

Visit https://www.glennamaynard.com/ for more information.

Never miss a new release sign up for my Newsletter

BB bookbub.com/profile/glenna-maynard

f facebook.com/groups/GlennasRebels

g goodreads.com/author/show/6903411.Glenna_Maynard

instagram.com/gchellewrites/

P pinterest.com/gchellewrites/

tiktok.com/@gchellewrites

Made in United States
North Haven, CT
13 August 2025

71605137R00090